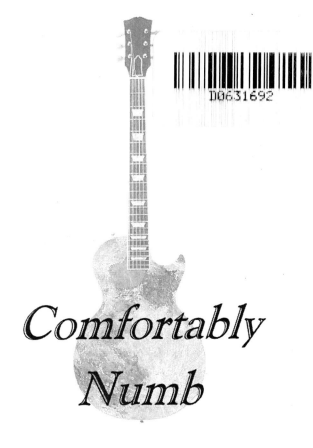

Comfortably
Numb

Books by Deborah Grabien

The JP Kinkaid Chronicles

Rock and Roll Never Forgets
While My Guitar Gently Weeps
London Calling
Graceland
Book of Days
Uncle John's Band
Dead Flowers
Comfortably Numb
Gimme Shelter *

The Haunted Ballads

The Weaver and the Factory Maid
The Famous Flower of Serving Men
Matty Groves
Cruel Sister
New-Slain Knight
Geordie *

Other Novels

Woman of Fire
Fire Queen
Plainsong
And Then Put Out the Light
Still Life With Devils
Dark's Tale

forthcoming

Comfortably Numb

Book #8 of the JP Kinkaid Chronicles

Deborah Grabien

Plus One Press
San Francisco

Plus One Press

COMFORTABLY NUMB. Copyright © 2013 by Deborah Grabien. All rights reserved. Printed in the United States of America. For information, address Plus One Press, 2885 Golden Gate Avenue, San Francisco, California, 94118.

www.plusonepress.com

Book Design by Plus One Press

Publisher's Cataloging-in-Publication Data

Grabien, Deborah.
    Comfortably numb : book #8 of the jp kinkaid chronicles / Deborah Grabien.—1st. Plus One Press ed.
        p. cm.
    ISBN: 0-9860085-1-6
    ISBN: 978-0-9860085-1-1
    1. Rock Musicians—Fiction. 2. Musical Fiction. 3. Murder—Fiction.
I. Title. II. Title: Comfortably Numb
    PS3557.R1145 C66 2013
    813'.54—dc22

                                                                2013908890

First Edition: November, 2013

10 9 8 7 6 5 4 3 2 1

Most of us are addicted to something.
This is for those of us who know it,
those of us who admit it, and
those of us who cope as best we can with those who know.

Acknowledgements

For everyone who gave me needed information about non-traditional, non-twelve step recovery and treatment programs and trends in current thinking, my heartfelt thanks.

All the nice wip-readers who keep it coming, book after book: Anne Weber, Marty Grabien, Sandra Larkin, and you know who you all are.

Deep thanks to the nice experts at Luxury Cars of Los Gatos, for letting me sit in the Bugatti Veyron and fiddle with things. That car goes to eleven.

And an acknowledgement of theft: Sandra Larkin came up with the phrase "Villa Priscilla" and I stole it. There, I said it in public.

Comfortably Numb

Chapter One

For some reason, the last few times I've got called over to the UK with no warning because something's come up that needs me there the day before yesterday, the timing's been absolute rubbish.

It's ridiculous. I always seem to get dragged off to England at just the times of year where anyone who wasn't off their nut would want to be anywhere but London: November, or February. I don't really need reminding as to why I don't live there anymore, but if I did, having to cross the Atlantic in midwinter, and then coping with sleety downpours and skies the colour of a nightmare about oblivion, would do it.

It might not have been quite so bad if we'd been out in the countryside. My last emergency trip over here had been for our long-time manager's funeral, a few years back now. Chris Fallow had been Blacklight's manager from the time he'd first seen Mac

Sharpe and Luke Hedley playing together as a folk duo. That goodbye had been made in a cold wintry garden, with Chris's widow Meg supported by the band and the extended band family. And yeah, the weather had been as miserable as it gets, but there'd been something nice about it, as well: Meg scattering Chris's ashes all over his own rose bushes, feeling he was there with us and watching his own memorial, had taken some of the bite out of the weather.

But this was London N10, a quiet little part of town right at the foot of Muswell Hill, and here it was, November again. Thanks to a heart check-up I hadn't been able to reschedule, I hadn't even been able to get over here with Bree in time for Guy Fawkes—we'd missed Bonfire Night by two days. Actually, now that I gave it some proper thought, Bree would probably find the whole Guy Fawkes thing morbid anyway...

"John?" Bree hadn't bothered glancing at any of the glossy magazines or the nice bland prints on the walls or the espresso machine. She also hadn't said a word about the fresh roses that must have cost someone quite a bit of dosh this time of year, since they had to have come out of a hothouse somewhere, and she loves roses. "Are you okay?"

"Yeah, I'm good." I shifted, trying to ease the tingles in my feet, and smiled at her. She was worrying about my multiple sclerosis or maybe my heart, something she does non-stop, basically. I couldn't complain about the sofa not being comfy; it was just as high-end as the rest of the room, big soft buttery leather, no buttons digging into your back or your arse. "Just still pissy I couldn't get you here in time to see the fireworks, that's all."

She smiled, but didn't say anything. There was no need to—I could practically hear her muttering "is *that* all?", even though she stayed quiet. She sighed, and relaxed. Easy to tell, with Bree: when she's tense, her shoulders go sky-high.

The waiting room was old-school Ye Olde Discreet Gent's

2

Club enough to set my teeth on edge. No expense spared, you know? It was very weird, realising I was responsible for this place's existence: I'd had the idea for it, paid for the leasehold on the property, funded everything from the staff to the espresso machine, arranged for it to continue to be funded, and told the people handling the details to put my first wife's name over the door, along with the words "Addiction Recovery Centre". The one thing I hadn't done was pay any attention to it, once it was up and running. I'd left that up to Blacklight Corporate. I'd never been near the place before.

"Mr. and Mrs. Kinkaid?" The voice came from behind the sofa. "I'm very sorry to keep have kept you waiting."

Bree and I both turned. We had to crane our necks to peer round the back of the sofa; someone, probably a twenty-year-old art school grad named Ludmilla or Veronique who specialised in designing oxygen bar interiors on the South Bank, had decided to face the sofa away from the main door. We hadn't heard the bloke come in or the door opening, either. The doors were as quiet and unobtrusive as the sofa and the espresso machine and the rest of the decor.

"Yeah, I'm John Kinkaid. This is my wife, Bree." We'd got up and gone round the proper end of the sofa, side by side. I held out my right hand; the left one was busy hanging on to Bree's. "Are you the director?"

He shook hands, nice easy grip, not too hard, not trying to prove anything. Good start, that was; I tend to judge blokes on how macho they think they have to get with a handshake. The ones who've got to show how tough they are, who've got some barnyard rubbish tied up in how hard they can squeeze someone else's hand, those are the ones I tend to avoid.

"Yes, I'm Robert Mourdain. Welcome to the Priscilla Kinkaid Addiction Recovery Centre."

He smiled suddenly, a real smile. Seemed like a pleasant type

3

all around, but you never know, do you? Besides, doing his gig, he'd have to wear a kind of mask, that whole persona thing. It comes with the territory. You can't help wondering how much is real. He looked too young to have the cred to be a director of anything, but that was probably genetics. "It seems rather ridiculous, me or anyone else welcoming you, of all people. I hope you were pointed at the espresso machine while you were waiting? A good cup of coffee on a day as raw as today can't be a bad thing."

"It can at my age, at least if I fancy sleeping." I'd got my right hand back with no damage done. "No caffeine for me past about three in the afternoon, I'm afraid, not unless I'm playing a gig that night."

I was still holding on to Bree's hand, swinging gently. Nice and warm. Good. She's got diabetes and her hands get icy cold even when she's someplace where it isn't pissing down a depressing sleet, or rattling windows with what sounds like icy pebbles whenever the wind kicks up. "No worries, we weren't waiting long at all. Ten minutes, maybe. Thanks for taking the time to show us round the place."

"It's a pleasure." He was holding the door open, but he shot me a sideways look. He'd sounded as if he really meant it, not just blowing the usual public-face smoke. "Actually, more of an honour. I've been a Blacklight fan since before I finished university in 1990—I still remember hearing some stuff on the radio and running out to get 'Backseat Babies'. I must have played that end to end about a hundred times. May I ask, are you going to tour again?"

"Don't know, not at this point." That answered one question about Robert Mourdain: he was older than he looked. If he'd got out of university in 1990, he had to be in his mid-forties at least, a year or two younger than Bree. "That last tour, *Book of Days*, was a killer. Two and a half years on the road, and I was quite ill at the end of it, for rather a long time."

4

"I know." He took a deep breath—it was pretty obvious he was deciding whether to say something. "My son Keith signed you in to hospital as a patient after your heart attack at Wembley. He'd been cursing his bad luck in having to work on the closing night of the tour, but he was damned glad to be there and able to do something, even if it was just handling the paperwork and making sure you were set up."

"Wow. Your son signed us in? Please thank him for us—the entire staff at the hospital was wonderful that night, and I never got a chance to really thank anyone personally."

Except for asking if I was okay, that was the first thing out of Bree's mouth since we'd got out of the hire car. Her hands might have been warm, and so was her tone of voice, but her shoulders were hunched up again, very tense. Most times, I've got no clue what's making her boulder up, but this time, it was pretty obvious: she didn't enjoy any reminders of the worst few weeks of her life, and anyway, it didn't matter how posh the waiting room was or how kind the director was, she was still standing in a building that had been named in memory of my first wife.

It didn't matter that the first wife in question had been a junkie and a panic killer and a suicide, you know? It didn't matter that she'd been dead a good long while, either. It made no difference that she and I had been so estranged for so long before she'd deliberately done enough heroin to take out a street gang, I probably could have passed her on the street and not looked twice. It had taken me a long time to sort out, but I did get it now: Cilla's name, no matter how or why it came up, was never going to mean anything but heartbreaking memories and bad associations for Bree.

We'd moved out of the waiting room, and into a nice long corridor. There was an odd split-personality thing going on there. One half reminded me of the long hallway in our house at 2828

5

Clay Street in San Francisco, all gleaming old wood panelling, but on the outer half, someone had done some serious remodelling or maybe just straight-up new construction: the wood was gone, replaced with glass walls floor to roof, ultra-modern. That let us get a view of what was probably quite a nice garden in the summer, surrounded on all four sides by the rest of the building, all three floors. There was a gardener out there, looking miserable and wet even in his boots and mac, pruning bits off dead things and putting them in a wheeled bin.

"That's the Quad." Mourdain sounded quite proud of it. Odd thing to get your peacock feathers up for, a bit of drab grass with some benches, but whatever. "On sunny days, our clients very often come out here and just think. It's a very nice place to meditate, and we do encourage meditation here, as part of the process. Ah, here we are—to the left, please? I wanted to show you our kitchen."

He pushed open a swinging door with a porthole window. Bree made a noise and I actually found myself grinning, first time since we'd walked in. My wife's a cook, and this kitchen was right up her *cul de sac*: tarted up to the nines, pots in long rows and a sodding huge stove. I counted eight burners.

"It's a very nice kitchen, isn't it?" Mourdain sounded polite, probably wondering why Bree'd reacted to it so hard. "We take food here very seriously. One of the things we stress in the recovery process is learning to love your body without whatever the artificial stimulus is, and that means a return to health. Proper food is a major component of that."

"No, Mr. Mourdain." Bree's red hair swung as she turned away from me. Oh, bloody hell. "Sorry, but you're wrong. It's not a major component, it's *the* major component. I know that if you've got an addictive personality you're going to be addicted to something one way or another, but most of it's negotiable. It's stuff you can do without just fine if you have to, and never really suffer

6

from the lack: sex, sports, money, heroin, tequila, shopping, whatever. But you try going without food for a few days, and you realise just how non-negotiable that is."

She sounded quite fierce, and I was biting back another grin, because Mourdain was blinking and looking as if his professional face might have just had a pie thrown at it. Of course, he didn't know Bree. I do.

"Yes, that's quite right, but I'm afraid I don't –"

"My wife's a chef." I dropped an arm around her. Yeah, so we were in the Priscilla Kinkaid Addiction Recovery Centre—it was Bree Kinkaid rocking the house, as usual. I'm quite proud of my old lady, you know? "She's got a cookbook coming out this year, about making sure people with special needs are properly fed. You ever want to talk food with Bree, you'd best know your stuff, because you're talking with an expert."

"Oh, I see." He'd gone back to doing the smooth thing. "A special needs cookbook? Excellent! Congratulations. Would you like to see the rest of the facility? As you know, we limit our guest residencies to no more than five clients at a time, so that we can give everyone specialised one-on-one care. And of course, our clients do tend to carry a certain weight of celebrity. The smaller list enables us to keep almost absolute control over the privacy concerns..."

We traipsed round the entire place, bedrooms, consultation rooms, public rooms, the lot. I found myself thinking I'd shown decent smarts, letting the staff at Blacklight Corporate handle all the details to do with buying a thirteen-room Victorian house in North London and get it remodelled for medical stuff and licensed for treating people with addictions they wanted to get clear of. The place had been updated to the nines, done to a turn; I'd told the Corporate Finance people handling it to spend whatever they needed to get it right. The staffing looked to be brilliant, as well, if Mourdain was anything to go by.

7

We finished up the tour, finally. I was beginning to feel a bit rough round the edges, probably from standing too long in one spot a few times too often over the past couple of hours. The multiple sclerosis gets beyond dodgy if I do that, and besides, it was time for my afternoon meds. I was ready to get back to our rented digs and have a cuppa and put my boots up. Bree, on the other hand, was looking and sounding energised.

"So, here's the important question." We were back in the front room, with the espresso machine and the leather sofa, saying our goodbyes and shaking hands. Bree and Mourdain were very much of a height, and they were meeting each other's eye. I'm a few inches shorter, myself, but I had his attention. "Are there any openings at the moment, or are you full up?"

"We do have one space open." He coughed, a delicate little clearing of the throat. "We actually have a waiting list, but when we received the call from Blacklight's corporate office about your visit, they asked us the same thing. We've just had a client check out—she finished her course of treatment—and we've held off on booking the slot. I'd rather assumed there was some need on a personal level."

He let the words trail away. Next to me, Bree'd gone stiff as a board. She'd got what he'd been thinking, all right.

"No, it's not either of us." I might not be eye to eye with him physically, but I know how to make people look at me when I need them to, and I was damned if I was having him thinking I'd fallen off the wagon on either booze or heroin after thirty years. "But yeah, a member of the extended band family's had a rough run the past year, and he's ready to walk away from it. Let's be clear, all right? He not only authorised us to discuss this with you, he's the one who asked us to check out the facility to see if he and his wife would be able to make a go of it while he dries out. From what I've seen here today, I'll tell him it's on. So yeah, hold that slot, and tell whoever handles the bookings, or whatever they're called, that sometime over the next couple of days, they'll probably be getting a call from a Mr. or Mrs. Mancuso."

When I'd told Robert Mourdain I had no clue whether Black-light was ever likely to tour again, I hadn't been dodging the question. I honestly didn't know.

The Book of Days tour was a couple of years in the past, now. Everything about that CD, about the tour we'd done to support it, had been completely out of our experience. We'd put out a nice little double CD and something about it had caught, big and hard. Next thing any of us knew, we'd been two and a half years dragging ourselves to every damned continent that had a venue big enough to hold huge crowds of screaming fans. It was nuts: the CD had swept the Grammy Awards, made us the first act to ever simultaneously hold down the number one, two and three spots on the charts, got us a gig at the Superbowl Halftime Show, and, thanks to his guest stint with Blacklight, had made Tony Mancuso into a multimillionaire with a drinking problem he hadn't had before. It had also turned Bree's hair mostly grey, courtesy of the massive heart attack I'd had the night of the tour closer.

So it was just as well no one in the band or our management seemed to be in any hurry to hit the studio or the road again just yet. The idea of another Blacklight tour hadn't crossed my mind in a good long time. Now that the subject had come up, though, I found myself looking at it. The idea wasn't thrilling me much, for quite a few reasons, not the least of which was the question of how in hell could we possibly top a CD that had not only shat-tered every existing record, but set a few of its own that weren't likely to get broken in my lifetime.

Also—hard to admit, but no more than the truth—we're not the kids we used to be. My local band at home in San Francisco is called the Fog City Geezers, but Blacklight's the same age.

Christ, I'm the youngest member and I'm up near sixty. Touring's hard work, yeah? Doesn't matter how luxe the hotels are, or whether you've got the band's name painted on the nose of the private jet, or any of that rubbish. If you're on the road, you're working, and working hard.

Still, if I said I wasn't missing working with Blacklight, I'd be lying. I love working with the Geezers, but they're different on every possible level, including the music itself. Blacklight's been making music as a band for over thirty years, and that's a good long time. Hard habit to break, yeah?

Bree and I held hands in the hire car. We weren't talking, just hanging out—that's one of the nice things about being together as long as we have, we don't have to constantly be talking. Bree actually dozed off; no surprise, really, since we were both coming off some serious jet lag.

She got a nice little nap, because it took a while to get back to our South London rental. We could have stayed closer to the Centre, if we'd wanted to: we still own our house at 18, Howard Crescent, just down the road from Muswell Hill, at the edge of Camden. It's quite a nice house, roomy and comfortable and close to the main business we were dealing with in London.

For Bree, though, the house wasn't so much a house as it was a nervous breakdown with built-in cupboards and cream paint. She hasn't got a single memory or association with the place that doesn't leave her shaking. Mac Sharpe, Blacklight's lead singer, had christened 18 Howard Crescent the "Villa Priscilla", and while that had got a laugh out of me, it wasn't really funny, because he'd nailed it; in Bree's head, the house belonged to my first wife, and Bree herself was always going to be miserable if we were anywhere near it. I was damned if I was having her upset, not if I could avoid it.

Besides, we'd both got quite fond of the mews house in South London we'd rented our last two visits. It's not huge or fancy, just a not too chichi little furnished holiday let with three up and three down, plus a functional kitchen and stairs that aren't too steep for me to deal with on a bad MS day. The furniture's dead simple, the garden at the back is tiny but very restful, and the place has got one loo and one bath, split in half. It's a nice location too, walkable to Knightsbridge and Sloane Square, quite close to Mac's place.

Mostly, though, it's what it hasn't got that we both like, and that's baggage. So far, the only personal history we'd had to cope with there had been the fallout from a nasty surprise left over from my first wife's drug habit. Bree'd accidentally jabbed herself with one of Cilla's old needles at the Camden house, during our honeymoon; we'd got the news that she hadn't caught AIDS or Hep C off it during our first stay at the mews house. We've got altogether too many shadows at our shoulders, me and Bree, and a few too many of them have something to do with 18, Howard Crescent.

Sitting in the car on the way back across the river, I slipped my hand free and got one arm round my wife. Bree made a gentle little noise, adjusted herself so that she wouldn't press up against the heartbeat regulator I've got implanted just under my left collarbone—and yeah, she's trained herself so that it's instinct now, and she really can do it in her sleep. She stayed nestled against me, breathing light and even, until the driver pulled up at the mews house.

"Wow." She gave a huge yawn. "God, how rude. Sorry about that. Stupid jetlag. Are we here?"

"Safe and sound. Got your key handy, love? No, not to worry, I've got mine." The driver was holding the door open for Bree; I slid out after her, and tipped the bloke. "Shit, I think the weather's got even worse."

"Well, we're closer to the river." Bree had her coat pulled tight. "I think I want some tea. It's that kind of day."

11

Once we'd got the door closed behind us and the weather shut out of doors where it belonged, I turned the central heating on and Bree headed for the kitchen. Funny thing—the kitchen here at the mews house was small, serviceable but nothing fancy. Back home in San Francisco, Bree's got a kitchen with top of the line everything: hanging racks of All-Clad cookware, big restaurant range with six burners, a Sub-Zero fridge. No expense spared, yeah? A professional chef's wet dream, basically. But she loves the mews kitchen. She says she can get comfy in there.

While Bree was setting out cups and pulling things out of the fridge for supper prep, I was checking the time. It's eight hours time difference, London to San Francisco. That meant it was nearing ten in the morning back home in California. Tony and Katia would be up by now, and anyway, I'd promised I'd ring as soon as I'd had enough of a look-around at the Centre to put an opinion together. No point putting it off.

Tony picked up on the second ring. "JP?"

"Oi, mate. Yeah, it's me." I watched Bree measure leaves into the tea ball. The poncey little shop in Kensington High Street had sworn this stuff was decaffeinated, and that had damned well better be true. I really didn't fancy being awake half the night, and these days, straight tea has the same effect on me as coffee does, after about three in the afternoon. "We're just back from being given the Grand Tour round the Centre. Nice little place I seem to be paying for."

"You don't like it?" His voice had sharpened up. *Shit.* He must have caught something in my tone.

"No, it's not that. It's just that I've got my own memories of rehab, and there's things I'd rather remember." *Yeah, like a couple of heart attacks and my last three MRIs. Or maybe a root canal or finding a dead body in a washroom.* "Actually, Tony, the place really is brilliant: everything top of the line, and a really competent bloke running the show. It's not a twelve-step thing, not at all. I was really specific about that when I first got this running. This is much more one on one. Seems to be more—I don't know, maybe holistic's the wrong word. I sent you the link, yeah? What's that motto thing they use?"

"'Meditation, conversation, realisation'." Interesting, that Tony seemed to have that one by heart. "I'll be straight with you, JP, I thought that sounded really corny—you know, some New Age woo-woo 'let's all contemplate our belly buttons and groove with our Inner Child' bullshit. But I got into reading what they offer, what their system's all about, and it reads really straight-up. Katia thinks so too." He paused, just long enough for a good long breath; I heard him inhale, coming across eight thousand or so miles and eight hours and the Atlantic Ocean. "So, be upfront with me, man. You think maybe these guys can help me clean up and get my shit back together? Because right now, I've been dry about three weeks but I'm not enough of a dumbass to think I can keep it up without help."

The electric kettle had boiled, and Bree'd got a nice little china pot loaded up and steeping. The kitchen filled up with a gorgeous smell, hints of Earl Grey and whatever else was in this particular blend. Outside, the wind was doing its best to get in round the edges of the window casements. If I owned this place, I'd pay someone a decent bit of dosh and let them do some serious work on the glazing...

"JP?"

"Yeah, still here." Bree was watching me, her chin propped in her hands. The kitchen was warming up around us, filling with the fragrant steam of tea, almost ready to drink. "We talked about this before, Tony. I'm not a doctor. I'm not even close to being any sort of expert. The only cred I've got is the fact that I've been through this myself, and all I can give you is what I think. For what it's worth, yeah, I do think they might be able to help you work it out. They seem to be into the whole body-mind-spirit-psyche deal, that you've got to feed and nourish all of it, because it's all connected. That just strikes me as commonsense, really."

"It's a solo thing, right?" He sounded anxious, suddenly. "I mean, it's not couples counselling or anything? I'd be in there on my own. Katia wouldn't be able to check in and be there with me. Right?"

"That's it, yeah, at least for the main part of the programme. I gather they do couples stuff after you've come through it. Makes sense, you know? Part of that whole 'heal the whole package' deal."

"Okay. Cool."

He sounded edgy, and I suddenly found myself wondering if the anxiety I'd heard was because he was afraid I'd say *no, not solitary, she'd be in there with you.* I could understand that, weirdly enough. Since I'd made myself look back at the month I'd spent in rehab all those years ago, I'd tried imagining how much harder it would have been with my old lady there with me. A thousand times, maybe ten thousand times harder. I couldn't even wrap my head around that idea: going through all that with Cilla, or Bree, sitting there watching? Not enough *oh fuck no* in the world for that one. Of course, it was possible Tony was at the other end of that, that he felt he needed Katia there for strength and support and backup while he was going through it. If that was it, I just hoped it wasn't a deal breaker.

"So do they have an opening right now? Should I call them?"

"They do, as a matter of fact. Soon as I'd had Blacklight Corporate ring them about it, they blocked off a spot. I think they thought it was for me, but not to worry, they know you're probably going to ring. The bloke in charge is called Robert Mourdain. He'll get you set up."

Bree pushed a cup of tea across the table at me, and got back up again, heading for the pile of foodstuff she'd got out for cooking. Not very interesting, only being able to hear my end of the conversation, but she knew the score, and she knew I'd fill her in. I keep as few secrets as possible from Bree, and I wouldn't on this one, anyway. Katia's her best friend, and knowing Katia as well as I do, there was no way in hell she'd be waiting back in San Francisco and flying out at the end of the month, or however long it was going to take. She'd be in London the whole time, and that meant Bree would be there as backup.

Listening to Tony filling Katia in, my phone suddenly beeped. "Tony, look, I need to go, it looks like Mac's on my call waiting. Ring me and let me know what we need to do at this end to get it together for you, all right—oi! Mac? That you? Damn, I've missed the call."

"He'll leave a message." Bree was chopping a bunch of fresh greens from Harrods's Food Halls. The knives here at the mews house hadn't been up to her standard—she's got a full set of Henckels, back in San Francisco—and she'd spent some serious money on decent cutlery. She says good knives are the first thing a cook has to have, to get the job done. "How's that tea? Do you need a refill?"

"No, I'm good. Still a bit too hot to drink—ah, there we go." The message tone chimed. I took a mouthful of tea and punched in my voicemail.

"*(beep) Johnny? Damn! I was rather hoping you'd be home and up for some conversation. Look, something's come up and I need to talk to you—well, to the entire band, actually. I've just got a call from Ali al-Wahid. He's about to open his new Emirates party palace or whatever it is, and he's offered Blacklight an ungodly amount of money to come out there and play the opening.*"

Chapter Two

In over thirty years of playing with Blacklight, I've been to more band meetings than I'd want to try counting.

Sometimes they're mellow, sometimes they're nuts, and sometimes you just turn up when they've told you to turn up, without the first clue as to what the fuck's going on. There's usually food, and generally a good bit of noise, not arguing, just making sure we all get heard. We're not much for rowing—the only one us with a temper worth mentioning is our drummer, Stu Corrigan— but we're rockers and we're not quiet, either.

The "all hands on deck, get your bums round to Fallow House at half past six sharp tonight and be next to a telephone if you're out of the country, and no argy-bargy about it from you lot" message that went out from our manager, Ian Hendry, the morning after the call from Mac wasn't new, either. He'd sounded almost as frazzled during the Book of Days tour, as it kept getting bigger and madder and the numbers kept climbing through the roof. But this, what Mac was proposing—Gordon *Bennett*. Yeah, definitely in the "what the fuck is going on" class.

Because Mac really was proposing it, or at least, that's the way it felt. I'd rung him back straightaway, once I'd got my wits back and stopped making gobbling noises at the phone.

That name he'd dropped, *Ali al-Wahid*, would have tripped every warning wire for anyone who'd been near the Book of Days tour. Ten people that we knew about, and possibly more, had died across a double handful of countries because of the bloke, or rather, because of his twin daughters. Nasty little bits of work those two were, Azra and Paksima al-Wahid. They were all dimples and flutters and coos and demure little headscarves and big soft eyes, and all the time they were getting up to things that managed to nearly shock even Mac. Top of their list seemed to be indulging their taste for rough sex. Not just basic rough, either; it wasn't about the "this is consensual, let's explore the limits" thing. We'd found out later their nasty little games had got people killed. They'd attached themselves to the tour, and while they were hitting the wrong sort of parties, they'd nearly taken Luke Hedley's stepdaughter Suzanne down with them.

The worst of it was, they had enough money to pay for what they wanted, and more than enough to climb into a bullet-proof limo and leave a huge sodding mess behind them for someone else to clean up. You don't run short of funds when your doting papa owns his own damned Emirate. They'd been banned from any access whatsoever to any future shows we did as a band, something that had been made clear to their dad by his old school chum, our lead singer, Malcolm Sharpe.

Of course, I'd told Bree about Mac's message. Me sitting there mumbling to myself, *is he joking, what the fuck, what, he's gone off his head* was unusual enough to get her attention in a hurry. I'd managed one short explanation—*remember the Tahini Twins, yeah well their dad wants to hire Blacklight to play the opening of his nasty little resort*—and that had been enough to get Bree gawking and muttering, right along with me. Like I said, there's no one did the Book of Days tour who wouldn't tense up hearing that particular family name, and that includes my old lady. So yeah, I'd rung Mac back straight away.

"Johnny, oh good, you're there."

"Yeah, I'm here. Mac, what the fuck, mate?"

"Oh, wait for it. You haven't heard anything yet, believe me." Odd thing—he didn't sound as if he'd suddenly gone off his head or anything. I mean, the whole tone of that voicemail, he'd sounded as if he actually wanted the band to do the show. And if he did, he'd have to have to have lost his mind. But he just sounded really focused and energised. "Let's keep it brief, all right? You're the first person to ring me back about this, and I expect everyone's pulling themselves off the floor right about now. My phone's probably going to light up like the doorway over a Vegas strip brothel, any minute."

"Okay." I settled myself back at the table. Bree'd abandoned any attempt at dinner prep for the moment; she'd slid into a chair opposite me, still looking stunned. "Mac, hang on, I'm putting this on the speakers. Bree's right here with me and I'm not having this conversation without her hearing it."

"Of course not. I wouldn't expect you to." He sounded amused. "I've got it on speaker at my end as well—Domitra's been sitting here asking if I know any good quiet hotels where I can go draw on the walls with crayons, since I've obviously left Victoria Station without the train. Ready? Good—Bree, angel, I'm probably taking you away from supper, but this won't take long. Now. Let's save some time, because I suspect that Ian's going to flip out and demand a full band meeting tomorrow anyway, and we can go over all the details then. Here's the abridged ver-

18

sion: Ali al-Wahid rang me—not Blacklight Corporate, me personally—and asked if Blacklight would consider playing two shows, back to back, to celebrate the opening of Give-Me-Your-Dosh-You-Stupid-Punter Island, or whatever he's christened this masterpiece of his."

"Bloody hell!" I remembered thinking, when we'd confronted al-Wahid, that he had all the arrogance that comes with money and power, but this was a mindfuck even by those standards. The bloke had the bollocks of a tyrannosaurus rex, to pull a stunt like this. "Mac, for Christ's sake, please tell me you told him to fuck off, all right?"

"I didn't. I was laughing too hard." Mac really did sound amused, but there was an edge to it. It suddenly occurred to me that he was just as pissed off by all that arrogance as I was. Nice, considering that Mac comes from money and prestige himself. "When I got my breath back, I told him that, in the first place, any offer of that kind should be made to our management and not to me directly, and that I didn't much fancy the Old School Tie rubbish. That in the second place, Blacklight was still on hiatus anyway, working on personal projects at the moment, and that we had no plans to change that status in the immediate future. And that oh, by the way, there's a third place and it's really the major consideration here, which is that the last time we had anything to do with him and his cultural stuff, we'd ended up with a drinks cooler full of severed hands from his little brats' fundamentalist bodyguards."

Across the table, Bree suddenly shuddered. I could see her remembering that night; it was right there in her face, that memory. I remembered that night myself, much too clearly: the roar and press of the crowd at Raymond Jones Stadium in Tampa as we'd done our two songs at the Superbowl Halftime Show. The plane back to the hotel in Miami. Everyone's phone suddenly lighting up with an anonymous link to the online version of Al-

Jazeera's English edition, about the mutilated bodies of two men having been found outside a nightclub in the Emirate of Manaar, with their hands missing, execution style. And then, getting back to the hotel, what we'd found waiting...

"He offered us five million pounds." Mac didn't sound quite as amused anymore. "I told him he might try cleaning his ears or maybe hiring some bodyguards to do it for him, assuming he had any left with hands still attached, because he would have to make that offer through our management, and by the way, I had no desire to play for someone who'd damaged my friends or the people I consider my family. Then I ended the conversation."

"Mac?" Bree was very pale, but she was smiling. "Just in case no one's told you this recently, you rock."

"Bree, angel, what a nice thing to say." Was that a snort I'd heard in the background? Right, Domitra Calley was there with him, his own bodyguard. She'd not only be snorting, she'd be rolling her eyes. "He rang back, about fifteen seconds later. Not a man who grasps being told to fuck off very easily, is Almanzor, but he's not completely stupid. He knows damned well the damage his misbegotten twins did, not to mention their damned bodyguards, and he's smart enough to have sussed out that it's Luke he'd primarily need to convince."

"Shit. Yeah, you're spot on about that. He's bloody arrogant, but he's not dim, not at all." I had an uneasy feeling in the pit of my stomach, suddenly. "Mac, you wanted to keep it brief. What's the upshot?"

"He doubled the price." Nice and crisp. "Ten million pounds for two nights work, all expenses covered of course, the lot. I said something quite rude and told him I was ringing off again, and then he made a very interesting offer to go along with the ten million quid. And unfortunately, it's not an offer I get to refuse out of hand, because it doesn't affect me. It affects Luke. And in any case, I've got an idea that's been moving round in my head for awhile now, and this actually—damn, and right on schedule, three incoming calls, oh lovely, it's Luke, Stu and Ian, bang bang bang. Johnny, I've got to go. Look for either a tight-arsed little message from Ian or else nothing at all, depending on how this goes. Cheers, bye."

He clicked off. Bree and I sat there, staring at each other. She was ash-pale, her hands locked together, her shoulders hunched hard. I reached across and covered her hands with mine.

"Bree, look." Her hands were chilly again. *Shit.* "I honestly do know how you feel. I promise, I do. I don't want to get within two time zones of Ali al-Wahid or his little opening night rave-up. But I tell you what, there's no point worrying about this one, not until we know more about it. Besides, I can always dig my heels in and tell them no, you know? How's your appetite doing, love? What were you thinking for dinner…?"

Mac had been right about the tight-arsed message from Ian, and the next evening, Bree and I headed over to Fallow House. Both of us were cold and both of us were hungry, since we hadn't really eaten after an early lunch. I hoped I'd been right when I told her not to worry about food, that the staff at Fallow House always made sure there was a meal brought in.

"Wow, what a nice house." Bree, wrapped up in her favourite cashmere coat, was standing on the pavement, staring up at Fallow while I paid the driver. "Georgian? Victorian? It looks so—I don't know, I guess festive is the word I want. All shiny and lit up. It's kind of Christmas tree-ish."

She was right. Heading up the front stairs together, I realised something: all the years we'd owned the place, I'd never done a night meeting there before. It had always been afternoon affairs, somewhere between one at the earliest and five at the latest. Ian was scrupulous about that, never expecting the band to give up their lie-ins every morning, and not wanting to drag us out of evening sessions or gigs or commitments. This meeting was a first.

21

There was a nice spread set out on the long mantel in what had once been some 19th century industrialist's posh dining room. I got myself a plate, made sure Bree was happy with the hot soup she was loading up on, and found us a couple of chairs. Half the band was already there, and while it was nice seeing Cal Wilson and Stu Corrigan, I was keeping my eyes open for the other half. I had the feeling that, whatever was about to go down, the beat wasn't getting set by the rhythm section this time. This whole thing, whatever it was, was centred on Mac and Luke.

Ian had already got Carla Fanucci, Blacklight's US Ops and PR manager, on the phone in LA. He was looking twitchy and cross though, and while I was listening for more arrivals, I got him to sit and talk for a moment. Turned out I'd been right about him being edgy: neither Patrick Ormand nor Tony had checked in, or responded to the meeting message. I had no clue what might be up with Patrick, but Tony was another story.

"Well—Tony might be travelling, Ian. He might even be in London by now, in fact."

"Tony's coming here?" Ian raised his brows at me. "What, that thing with your recovery centre, that worked out for him, then? Glad to hear that."

Right then, I gave up trying to be delicate about Tony's situation. If the band was thinking about asking him to do anything, we were all going to need to know what was happening. That's how Blacklight works. "Yeah," I told Ian. "That's it. Now I think about it, he's probably not here yet, because Katia hasn't rung Bree. Thing is, Ian, I'm damned if I see why it would matter. From what I heard last night, talking to Mac, this thing with Ali al-Wahid is all rubbish anyway. The bloke fucked us over. Shit, we lost family because of him. We don't need the money. Why would anyone even be considering playing a show for this self-entitled pillock?"

"I don't know, JP." There it was, the core of why his knickers were in such a twist: lack of information. Ian's entire gig is based on him being not only on top of every detail of the situation in question, but having at least a few strands of things yet to come under control. He doesn't like not knowing things. "All I know is that Mac is considering it, and so is Luke. Mac says he'll tell us everything when—right, they're here. Brilliant. Let's get this started."

As soon as the band's two founders walked in, I knew something major was up. Mac had brought Dom with him—he rarely leaves home without his bodyguard—but Luke was alone, and that was a dead giveaway as to just how iffy this was likely to be. He rarely leaves Karen behind, and the idea that he'd left her out of this meeting in particular brought it home, good and hard: her daughter had got into some serious shit because of Ali al-Wahid. So something was up, it was tricky, and it was big.

"Hey." Domitra nodded at us, and made for the food. She's a carb-loader, mostly; she says she needs a lot of carbohydrates to keep her fighting weight up. You'd have thought raw meat would be more her style, but no, she likes rice and quinoa and things like that. "Good, they've got hot food. Shitty weather out there. You maybe going to try to talk some sense into my boss? Because I can't get anywhere and he's pissing me off."

"Kind of tricky, since I don't know what he's going to say." Bree'd finished her soup. She was watching Mac. Luke was right behind him, and I'll tell you what, I'm closer to Luke than I am to most people, but I had no clue what he was thinking or feeling just then. He was completely on guard.

"Thank you, Bree. Rather nice, not being screamed at or called a lunatic. It's the first time today—well, almost the first time." Mac had everyone's attention. He's good at that, but no surprise; it's his job. "Look, let's get this out and at least into everyone's mental circuitry, all right? You all know that Ali al-Wahid rang and offered Blacklight ten million pounds to play two nights to open

23

his sheikh casino, or whatever it is. I told him to fuck right on along, and he came back with an addition to the ten million. He's offering matching funds—ten million quid, not exactly pocket change—to the Foundation for Research into Diabetes."

Oh, bloody hell.

That explained why Mac had felt this one was over to Luke to decide. It also explained why he'd left Karen at home. Luke's second wife has diabetes, and not Bree's kind, either. Bree's got type 2. She takes pills and watches her diet; her pancreas is impaired. But it's not dead, and Karen's is. Karen's a type 1 diabetic, no natural insulin produced at all. She's always hooked up to her pump, having her insulin and blood glucose levels regulated by this little portable machine she has to stay attached to. And Type 1 comes with some really scary side issues, like an increased risk of things like liver and pancreatic cancer. Bree's is bad enough, but it's nowhere near as bad as Karen's.

The Foundation was the charity Luke had founded to raise awareness and money for research, specifically into Type 1. And he'd just been offered ten million quid as a donation, with the only strings attached apparently being that the entire band showed up and played the opening party.

I caught Bree's eye. We had one of those moments of marital synchronicity, both of us thinking the same thing and knowing it: *no wonder Luke didn't bring Karen. It would have made it impossible for anyone to say no…*

"There's a bit more." Mac wasn't done yet, and Luke wasn't interrupting, either. "I've had an idea in my head, just the seed of one really, for a few months now. I didn't want to bring it up while Johnny was launching the Geezers' first CD, and of course not while he was touring the band. But now that we're all here, and all off the road, here's the thing: am I the only one who thinks we really ought to play a few big free shows, as a thank-you to the Blacklight fan base? Because let's face it, we're not getting any younger. I've got some new material and I quite like it, but it would be well beyond miraculous for it to do something that hit the way Book of Days did. I've got no desire at all to do another major tour at this point, but maybe something like three or four free festival dates, one here, one somewhere on the continent, and one in North America—opening acts, the whole thing. Anyone?"

"I like it." That was Cal, and when I turned his way, I saw Stu nodding as well. "So long as it was planned out well in advance, and so long as we all agreed it would be just a few dates. I don't want a major tour either, but yeah, I've been thinking about the fan base recently. The website's getting more questions about that from the fans every day, I'm told."

"I'm good with it, as well." I'd got hold of Bree's hand. "No major tour for me either. Not saying that's forever, but for now, no tours. Still, a kind of private prezzie to the fans? Fuck yeah, I like that. What I don't see, though, is what this has to do with playing for your old mate from university. Care to clue us in, Mac?"

He grinned suddenly. It was a damned good thing none of the fans were there to see that grin, especially the female fans. It was as dark and as cheeky as it gets. Behind him, Luke had a grin on that was a good deal darker. Whatever Mac had in mind, Luke already knew all about it, and approved.

"Clever lad, Johnny. I've costed out three weekend-long festival dates, three specific sites in mind. With full outdoor rig, permits, the usual facilities and then some, paying our people and everything else, it works out to right around nine million pounds." He must have seen the light going on for the rest of us, because the grin got even cheekier. "I say let's tell Ali we'll do it for twelve million, one show only. Plus, he makes that ten million gift to Luke's foundation, and agrees to put another two million into the Kinkaid Recovery Centre, to make it an even twelve

25

million in matching funds. He gets to make himself feel better about what his little twin hell spawn did, we get to do something good for the fans, and everybody wins. I say let's get him to pay for the whole damned thing."

"So this idea of Mac's—do you really want to do it?"

"I'd rather do you, actually."

"Smartass." She was practically purring. "But seriously, John…"

"Yeah, I know, I just did. Give me a few minutes, maybe we can try for an encore." I had both arms draped over my wife, and her naked back up against me. I planted a lazy kiss on the nape of her neck, and tasted salt. "You taste like a potato crisp. You talking about this little do in Arabia, Bree?"

It was late, well past one in the morning. The BBC weather service had said there was a hard freeze likely, and maybe some snow as well. That was easy to believe; outside the bedroom window, the moon had a sort of icy nimbus round it. It looked colder than usual, somehow. There were a few stars out, and they looked like frost points out there in the distance.

"An encore sounds good, but you might have to wake me up first, unless you've got some secret necrophilia thing I don't know about. I'm as limp as overcooked vermicelli." She wasn't joking; she was thoroughly relaxed. "No, not the thing in Manaar. I know you're not thrilled at the idea of doing that. I kind of got the impression that no one was, except Mac. Would it really be that hard to turn down the money?"

"Not for me, it wouldn't." Between the blast-furnace heat the small of her back was giving off and the duvet we were snuggled under, I was getting rather drowsy myself. Of course, some of that was pure physics: there'd been a very intense half-hour of slap and tickle in there, as well. "I mean, right, it's a lot of money. But if you want the truth, I think the idea of making al-Wahid pay

26

through his posh self-entitled nose for the privilege is what's turning Mac on. If you weren't talking about the Manaar deal, what were—oh, right, that whole thing about doing a few festival dates for the fan base. That what you meant, love?"

"Mmmm. Yep." She rolled over, facing me. "I hate to say it, but when Mac was talking about it, it sounded like something most of you wouldn't touch with a barge pole. I mean, I guess it's possible that I'm picturing something that doesn't have any resemblance to what Mac's suggesting..." Her voice trailed off; I'd got one hand on a sensitive bit of her, and tweaked lightly. I know where her buttons are, and right then, I was more in a mood to take her places than to talk. "Wow. Um. Okay, maybe I'm not as limp as overcooked vermicelli..."

"Good job," I told her, and pinned her on her back. "As it happens, neither am I. Here we go..."

Fifteen minutes, and that turned out to be quite a nice little encore. You'd think that with me being sixty, we'd be less intense about this part of being married, but not at all. I think I get a bigger rush from feeling her holding on to me like a drowning woman than I did when she was twenty. Not the way most romance novelists and whatnot would have it, but there you go. We've never been typical, me and Bree.

"Hello, darling." I bit her ear, a tiny little nip. Nice thing about being belly to belly horizontally instead of vertically is that the height difference, her being two inches taller than I am, doesn't matter. Lying with her under me, I can reach her earlobe just fine, and I did. She wriggled a bit, but this time, she really had gone pretty limp. Good. That's part of my job, getting her there. "So what were you seeing? Woodstock or the Us Festival or Glastonbury?"

"What was I—oh, right, Mac's thing. I forgot." Even in the darkness, I could see her eyes had gone cloudy, with sleep or pleasure, or maybe both. "Sort of, I guess. Just a lot of mud, and dirty port-a-potties, and what happens if it rains? I mean, the fans probably wouldn't mind too much, or at least they'd put up with it for a chance to see a free Blacklight show. But, well, you'd mind. Wouldn't you?"

I grinned down at her. "Fuck yes. What, you think I'm sleeping out with the mice and the bunnies in an unplanted alfalfa field somewhere in Belgium? At my age? Not a chance. We'd have a good hotel booked and helicopters to take us there—what, Bree?" She'd twitched a bit, and made a noise. It wasn't a particularly happy noise, either.

"That's nice for us. But what about the fans?" Suddenly I wasn't quite so relaxed anymore, myself. I knew the tone in her voice: it was Bree's Conscience, that fierce crusading thing she gets. "Isn't the whole point supposed to be that you guys would be doing this for them? I know a lot of the fan base is younger, especially after *Book of Days*, but a lot of them are our age, John. I'm only just about to turn fifty and the idea of sleeping in the middle of a muddy field for the weekend—oh hell no. Really not. How would people in their sixties cope with that? And is it fair to even ask them to do it?"

"Good point." I rolled off her. The tickybox in my chest, the weird little device that keeps the electrical impulses to my heart where they're supposed to be and keeps me out of a coffin for the time being, ramped up, settled, and then eased off. "That, well, I couldn't tell you, love. The logistics aren't handled by the band—never have been. That's management's call. We get input, of course we do, but we're not in on the details, how things like the facilities get handled."

She was quiet. There wasn't much light in the room, but I didn't need it. I'd know she was worrying, even with a blindfold on. Time to ease that up; otherwise, she'd sleep badly and I wasn't having that, not over something like this.

"No point in worrying about that, Bree, not yet, anyway. Right now, it's just a pretty idea that's being looked at. And have a little trust in the band's brain trust, okay? They've never let the fans down before, and I don't see Ian or Carla or David Walters doing that now, you know?"

"True." She sighed, nice and easy. Good, that was tension on its way out. "Damn, I'm sleepy. It looks really cold out there—there's something about this weather that just knocks me sideways. It makes me want to sleep and sleep and sleep." She leaned forward and kissed the back of my shoulder. "'night, baby."

Yeah, well, maybe she was sleepy. Unfortunately, that question she'd put up, about being fair to the fans, had got into my head, and it wasn't giving an inch. Mulling it around in my head, ways to throw a huge free outdoor festival party for a couple of million people and have them remember the music instead of the smelly chemical toilets and the mud, cost me a good hour's worth of kip. That happens quite often at our house. Bree's conscience kicks in, she gets fierce, I get soothing or practical, she agrees with me and passes out, and I'm the one left lying awake, listening to the gears in my head churning on about whatever she threw out there before she went off to share a kitchen with Julia Child in Paris in the 1960s, or whatever she was dreaming about.

She let me sleep in next morning, which was just as well. The multiple sclerosis doesn't like temperature extremes, or humidity, either. Even if the weather isn't causing a full-on exacerbation or relapse, it makes its presence felt: the ataxia gets worse, for one thing, the shakes in my legs and hands getting much more pronounced. Things that are normally reasonably easy to cope with, all the small background pains and tingles, get sharper. They're more there, somehow.

And of course, there are times when I get caught in a combination of things—time zone changes, weather, exhaustion—when the disease says *right, you fucking clot, you've bummed this up completely and now you get to be useless and miserable until I say*

29

otherwise, so grit your teeth because I'm going to get on with it. So when I did wake up, just after ten next morning, I probably shouldn't have been surprised when the first tentative stretch of my right leg and foot left me swearing under my breath and reaching for my right calf. The entire leg had reacted to the stretch by pretending it had been doused in petrol and hit with the business end of a blowtorch. That's what it felt like, anyway.

I lay there for a few minutes, gritting my teeth, waiting for things to settle down enough for me to suss out where the rest of the bad bits were likely to be. It didn't work, that strategy—the whole body seemed to be in an uproar. And Bree'd gone downstairs, probably a good hour before.

Shit. I needed my meds, and an extra hit of painkiller probably wasn't a bad idea, either. I also needed a piss, and right now, I wasn't sure my legs were getting me across the room into the split loo. Right. Call her, let her know…

"Bree?"

Yeah, well, that was a mistake. My jaw had locked up on the left side, trigeminal neuralgia, one of my least favourite side effects of this bloody disease. I could barely talk, and I wasn't trusting my legs, either. The only thing that seemed to be working was my damned bladder.

Ring her, Johnny. She's got her cell with her, she always does. Ring her. Yours is right there.

I managed to fumble the cell off the table and into both hands without dropping it. The noise my bladder was making was putting pictures into my head, of things like tsunamis and hurricane storm surges and very large dams. I got the phone flipped open and spared a moment of gratitude for speed dial. All I had to do was punch in the number 1…

"*(beep) This is Bree Kinkaid, I'm sorry but I'm unavailable at the moment, please leave a name and number and a brief message at the tone, and I'll get back to you as soon as I possibly can —*"

It was almost funny, you know? She was right downstairs, probably in the kitchen, and probably on the phone with someone else. And that meant I was going to have to get across the room and into the loo somehow, because the bladder had run out of patience, or room, or both.

I was halfway between the bed and the door when I heard her coming upstairs, and heading for me. The fates had decided to cut me a break, apparently, and thank Christ for it.

"John? Are you awake? I just got a call—oh shit, shit, shit, baby I'm sorry, why didn't you call me!"

"Did." My jaw was locked up tight, but she was here, and helping me into the loo, and getting my meds together. I know she couldn't possibly have done all that without ever letting go of me—she's not Superwoman, not really—but it felt as if that's what she'd done. I sat, and winced; the toilet seat was chilly. "Voicemail."

"I was on the phone. Katia called." She handed me a small pharmacy's worth of pills and a cup of water. "Here, take these while you're sitting. I'll help you back to bed when you're done. Okay? Do you think you could handle some breakfast? Maybe something soft, or a cup of tea…?"

We got me back to bed, finally. The meds were helping a lot faster than they usually seem to work, and I got a hand out just as Bree looked to be getting up, and rested it on her arm.

"You said—Katia? Tony here?" The words came out almost slurred. Christ, I sounded like a fucking stroke victim, but inside my head, the brain was going rapid-fire: *need to let Tony know about al-Wahid's offer, no not yet, need to check with the rest of the band first and see if they want to ask him, he's not really a member of Blacklight but for this gig he should play, bloody hell Johnny, you're not asking anyone anything until this little lot eases up.*

"They're both here. Katia said their plane got in last night. Tony hasn't checked himself into the Recovery Centre, though, not yet." She took a long breath. "He says he wants to talk to you about it before he does that. I don't really know what's going on—Katia was being sort of careful, and cagey. You know the way she gets, when she's talking about Tony and doesn't want him to know it?"

"Yeah." I'd nearly nodded, but stopped myself in time. When the trigeminal thing hits, nodding leaves me feeling like Marie Antoinette about a nanosecond after the executioner let go of the lever. "And?"

"I'm not really sure. From something Katia said, Tony actually went over there this morning and spoke to the director, the guy we met, Robert Mourdain. And I don't know what's going on, John, but from what I got from Katia, there's some kind of complication, and Tony says he isn't checking in until he talks to you first."

Chapter Three

During the past thirty years, we've had Tony and Katia over to dinner more times than I can count. This time, though, we had a couple of firsts: Bree'd never cooked for them in London before, and usually, when the MS is giving me grief, she keeps people out of the house as if she were that pissy three-headed dog thing, the one that guards the gates of Hell. That night, though, we broke the usual rules, and a couple more besides.

Middle of the afternoon, after Bree'd rung Katia back and got them to come over for a meal, we'd done another first: I'd asked Bree to please talk to Ian for me, and get some details about what was being discussed by the band and our management. Bree spent most of her life shying away from the working end of my life, and even now, married and settled and nothing to keep her from it, she's still not comfortable with it. I hated having to ask the favour, but I hadn't got a choice: I needed the information before I talked to Tony about anything at all, and talking to Tony or anyone else meant giving the neuralgia a shot at dying down before Tony and Katia got here.

Bree agreed to do it, without any sort of fuss. She didn't even ask me why. It was right out of character for her, but she knew what was needed, and why I was asking her to do it. She just nodded, and reached for my phone. She doesn't keep band management numbers programmed into her own cell.

It was a short conversation, without one wasted word. She got Ian on the line, explained what was happening with the MS and why I wasn't ringing myself, and then just got on with it.

"Ian, look. John's worried. Tony and Katia are coming over here later, to talk with John about Tony checking into rehab." She had her eyes fixed on my face. I nodded, a tiny little movement of my head, pushing the pain away, not letting her see it: *good, yeah, keep going love, you're doing great.* "Hold on a second, I'm putting the speaker on, so that John can listen in. The main thing is, is there anything we ought to know about the show in Manaar?"

"You mean, about whether there's been any decisions made?" Ian sounded gruff and harassed, but he usually does. "Or about whether we'd ask Tony to come play the show if it does go down? Oi, JP, hope you feel better soon."

"Both." Like I said, Bree wasn't wasting words.

"Nothing's decided." Ian wasn't wasting words, either, apparently. "I'd have rung JP or emailed him—we'd need his yea or nay. That's how Blacklight works. I got the formal proposal this morning. I can tell you Mac and Luke are both up for doing it as a one-off, making it contingent on matching donations from al-Wahid to JP and Luke's non-profits. One thing I can say definitely is that, if it does go down, we'd be asking Tony. The proposal's very clear that the personnel who played the Book of Days tour is the lineup wanted. Anything else?"

Bree looked me. I mouthed one word at her: *when?*

"Ian? John wants to know when that show would be happening, if it does go down. And is it just one show? Because Mac said two, originally."

"One show, New Year's Eve. Manaar al-Wahid opens New Year's Day. And no, don't ask me if he named his little boogie palace after himself—Mac says his name means 'lighthouse' in Arabic."

I blinked at Bree. The thought must have been pretty clear in my face; I didn't care a rat's arse about what the place was called, it was the timing that was worrying me. New Year's was just about seven weeks away, and the full course at the Recovery Centre, including the couples counselling, ran about five. And we hadn't even officially decided to do it yet...

"Okay. Ian, John's gesturing at me, and I'm guessing that means he's thinking the same thing I am, that things are going to get shaved really close." Her voice went crisp, suddenly. "And that means he'll stress over it, which makes the MS worse, which makes everyone's life harder. So let's save some time."

I was watching her. I had no clue, honestly, what was going on in her head, or what she was going to say next.

"John?" She'd turned to face me, getting us eye to eye. "I don't want to push, but can you give Ian a thumbs up or thumbs down right now? If the rest of the band says yes, are you up for doing the show, without or without the insane time scheduling? And after that, I need to get off the phone and go get some groceries. I can't cook dinner with nothing in the house."

"Yes." Bless those painkillers, they're good stuff. I could almost talk without wincing. Not much volume in there, and not a lot of breath, but it was easing up. Ian and Bree could both hear me, and that's what mattered just then. "Thumbs up."

"Good. I'll let the rest of the band know." He paused, just barely, but enough for us both to notice. Same old Ian, gruff and to the point. "Thanks, Bree. Saves us all a lot of time and work, you ringing me. Feel better, JP."

He rang off. Bree and I were left looking at each other. Neither of us was saying anything, not yet.

New Year's Eve. That meant seven weeks for the band to agree to do it at all, sign contracts, get our crew together, agree on a set list, get into rehearsals. Seven weeks for Ronan, our sound designer, to get out to the site, scope it top to bottom. Seven weeks to get a set designed, get the gear over there, get the fucking thing built.

And for five of those weeks, it looked as if Tony wasn't going to be available for anything at all, not even to approve or disapprove of things. That was part of the deal. Mourdain had made it clear: the first few weeks of the process, Tony stayed in and the outside world stayed out. No exceptions, not even for Katia, and if Katia was excluded, so was the band.

Bree kept dinner, and the shopping for it, really simple that night: she rang for a hire car, had the driver wait while she hit the Food Halls at Harrods, and came straight back again. By the time she came up to get me at a quarter of six, the relapse had eased enough for me to get up on my own and even get a quick hot shower. I'd dried off and got dressed, and was actually putting my shoes on when she opened the bedroom door to tell me Katia'd rung to say that she and Tony were planning on getting here right round a quarter past six.

The smell of supper cooking hit me full-on as I got to the head of the stair. I've spent a lot of nights in a house that smells like Bree's cookery, but that smell, that night, stopped me in my tracks.

"John?" She'd stopped as well, right behind me, sounding worried. "Are you okay? What's the matter?"

"No, I'm fine." I closed my eyes and inhaled, savouring it, wondering why the smell of something in the oven should be having this effect on me, and having it this strongly. I could talk now, not much pain in there at all. "It's just something about whatever you've got in the oven, that's all. I was about ten years old for a couple of seconds, there. Brought me straight back to my mum's kitchen, Christmas or Boxing Day dinner, I think. What are we having, Bree?"

"Best Scotch topside roast. Roasted potatoes and Yorkshire pudding. Runner beans. I didn't make the puddings from scratch—no time. They'd better be decent or I swear, I'll take them back to Harrods and throw them at the cashier."

"They'll be brilliant, not to worry."

I started downstairs. Funny thing, how what you smell and where you smell it can play off each other. Bree'd probably done a hundred roasts in the big Viking at home in San Francisco in her day, maybe more. A roast smells like a roast, you know? Somehow, though, none of them had taken me this way, dragging me back fifty years to our tidy little house in South London, me knowing there'd be roast beef for supper, listening to the sizzle of my mum's Yorkshire puds in the hot fat, smelling the meat and the potatoes, wondering if I could hide the soggy boiled runner beans under something without letting on I hadn't eaten them, and still get a sweet for afters.

We didn't have a lot of money, back when I was a kid. My dad was a sign maker for a local firm, non-union, nice people but they couldn't pay him much. Me being an only child, after my baby brother died, was probably the only thing that kept decent food on the table night after night, at least until I was fifteen and started playing sessions, with my dad signing official approval for me to do it.

Not a big family, just the three of us, and not a lot of money for fancy touches. A roast in the oven, when I was a kid, meant either a birthday or a holiday. It was a treat, something special, something to be remembered.

Maybe you have to be where you first started, physically that is, for the smell to hit that hard. Either that, or there's some difference in the way the meat smells on either side of the pond. Whatever—I don't know. But I was still feeling warm and mellow when Tony and Katia arrived, a few minutes early.

Bree was paying attention to the runner beans, tossing them in a pan with a steamer piece in it, to make sure they stayed crisp and cooked evenly. She's never served up soggy veg in her life. I headed down the hall to let the Mancusos in. The mews house hasn't got anything in the way of an overhang, so whatever the weather was doing, it was doing it all over them until someone let them come indoors, out of the night.

A cold blast of wind hit me as I got one hip against the door, and it damned near pushed the pair of them inside. I got a quick hug from Tony, which surprised me. We're not touchy sorts, either of us.

"Oi mate, you're looking bedraggled. Not exactly the best time of year for London weather."

"Yeah, I noticed." He slid out of his topcoat, and watched me dig out a hanger for it. Katia had already murmured a fast hello, and headed down the hall towards the kitchen. Even not having been here before, she knows that, when the house smells like food, just follow the smell if you want to find Bree. "Man, last time I was someplace this cold, it was back in Moscow, for Book of Days. Fucking icebox out there, except iceboxes don't come with wind. You stay inside all day? Smart move, JP."

"Not much choice, really. Most of the day, I was down with the MS." I lifted an eyebrow at him, and lowered my voice. "Tony, anything you want to talk about privately, just you and me? Because now's the time to do it."

He met my eye, and I felt myself relax. That look was a question answered, one I hadn't fancied asking myself. Because yeah, he really did look bedraggled, but not the way he'd looked when

38

he'd walked into our suite at the Beverly Wilshire earlier in the year, the wrong side of a two-day drunk, reeking of stale tequila, on his own because Katia'd broken under the strain and walked out. He was tired, a bit puffy, but his eyes were clear. This wasn't stale-drunk, it was just jetlag and stress, and yeah, believe me, I know the difference.

"No," he told me. "Everything I need to talk to you about, I've already talked over with Katia. And if Katia gets to hear it and you get to hear it, so does Bree."

I waited. Down the hall, I heard the murmur of the women's voices, and the funny little *clack* the oven door gives, if you let it bounce on its springs. Bree must have taken supper out of the oven, and was letting it settle, or rest, or whatever it's called. If this was our London house, properly ours and not just a rental, we'd be replacing that oven with a decent one...

"Katia's been amazing." The words came out in a rush, and I jerked my head round towards him. "She's been right there, no judgements, no bullshit. She's been nagging my ass when it needed nagging and letting me cry all over her when it got too rough. She's been a rock. What the fuck, JP, how long has she been doing this, and how come I never noticed before? What are you laughing at?"

"Nothing. Just a bit of *deja vu*, that's all. If you're good to go, let's have some supper. There's something I need to talk to you about—band business."

Supper tasted as good as it smelled. We ploughed through the meat, the potatoes, all of it—no bread, not that night, because we had the Yorkshire puds, and really, that's what they are, a kind of biscuit cooked in drippings. The roast was done to a turn, nice and tender, which meant I could actually chew it; after an MS relapse, it's a toss-up. Everyone ate quite a lot, including Tony. He had a third helping, in fact. That was more confirmation, if I'd needed it, that he was still dry.

"Oh yum." Katia was trying not to belch. "Was that Ye Olde Roast Beef of Olde England? Because if it is, then I don't get all those clichés about how bad English food is. *So good.* Bree, is there a dishwasher? Do you need help cleaning up?"

"No, that's okay." Bree'd started loading dishes into the sink. "I'll let them soak until later. I want to get you guys back to your hotel early—you said you were still jetlagged."

"Seriously." Tony yawned suddenly. "Wow, I'm full. Killer dinner. Thanks, Bree. JP, you said you had band business you wanted to talk to me about? Which band? The Fog City Geezers?"

"No. Blacklight business."

I caught them up on the story, all the details right through Bree's call to Ian. Bree was setting out teacups and filling the kettle. "…and yeah, if this is happening, you'll be asked to come play it. I don't know how a share would work out, since Mac's looking to take most of the pile and use it to throw a few parties for our fan base, but I'm sure something could be worked out. That's if you wanted to come play, of course. And that's if it even happens."

"I'm not worried about the money." His brows were bunched. "I'm just—did you say New Year's?"

"Yeah, I did, and yeah, that could make the timing tricky. Even assuming you got started at the Centre tomorrow, it would be shaving things right down to the bone for time. But first things first: do you want to do it, if it goes down?"

He grinned. "Fuck yes. Are you nuts? I wouldn't miss it. And boy oh boy, how devious is Mac?" The grin faded. "But I haven't signed in to the Centre yet. There's—there might be an issue. Look, JP, I know you put a lot of money into this thing, but I need to ask you: Can you absolutely vouch for their discretion? Are you positive, I mean really positive, about the privacy factor?"

Bree had set cups out, and poured boiling water into her favourite pot. The women had gone quiet, listening. Whatever had got Tony asking me that question, of any question he could have put to me, Katia knew all about it.

"I can't vouch for that absolutely, Tony, can I? I'm not God, or something. I can tell you privacy's a high priority there, one of their highest, that they emphasise it, that it was something I insisted on when it was being set up and when people were being hired. The entire thing would fall down without that. And Mourdain gets it, about the celebrity thing. Why?"

"I went over there today." He was stirring his tea, choosing his words, being very careful. "I met the director. Nice guy, scary smart, all the right stuff, just like you described him. He showed me around the place, the rooms, the gym, everything, even the garden."

He stopped. Bree and I were both watching him. Katia wasn't—she was watching me, weirdly enough.

"There was someone out in the garden." He took a mouthful of tea. "Katia'd gone to use the bathroom, it was just me and Mourdain. Mourdain got me back inside in a hurry—I guess they weren't expecting anyone in their right mind to be out in that weather, freezing their ass off. Obviously, it was one of their clients, someone who's resident at the moment. But it was too late. We'd seen each other."

"Wow." I shook my head. Inside, I was swearing. I was going to have a few pointed words for the director about that one. "Sorry about that, mate, but I don't see how Mourdain could have helped that. You afraid that whoever it was recognised you?"

"I know damned well he did." Tony took a breath. "We recognised each other. You'd have recognised him too."

It was probably just as well that, even with a lot of my head concentrated on Tony's situation, I'd already sorted out and accepted that Blacklight was going to play the Manaar show. Considering how tight the timing was, it wasn't as if I had a lot of room to dither about it.

If it had just been a question of getting a show together, seven weeks would have been no problem at all. Blacklight's got one of the best crews on earth, and the most stellar sound and stage design teams you could hope to find, in Ronan Greene and Nial Laybourne. We've done short-notice gigs before, quite a few of them. Mac's always been big on fundraisers, and those tend to be last-minute affairs. That makes sense, since it's usually some sort of emergency prompting the need for them in the first place. Hell, I'd met Bree for the first time at a hurricane relief benefit in San Francisco that had been pulled together perfectly in about three days. And more recently, just a few years ago, Ronan and Nial had got the band onstage for a free show at Frejus, in the South of France, in less than a week.

But this was a different situation entirely, in a different league, and there was no point trying to pretend it wasn't. I didn't have the projection numbers yet, those were probably coming at tomorrow's meeting, but there was no getting away from the bottom line. Almanzor al-Wahid wasn't about to hand over twenty four million quid unless the show he was expecting was fucking huge.

Then there was the issue of rehearsals. When we'd done the Frejus gig at the Cannes Film Festival, the band had just come off a few weeks working in the studio together, eight hours a day. We'd had our timing down, and everything was fresh and tight. But Blacklight hadn't done anything as a band since Book of Days had ended, and that meant we hadn't played together for a couple of years. Doesn't matter how much of a pro you are, or how long you've been playing together: once you lay off gigging and rehearsing for a while, there's going to be some rust that needs to be polished off the edges.

But the biggest issue was the situation with Tony. The last thing he'd told us, before he and Katia had climbed into the hire car, was that he was signing himself into the Centre in the morning. He'd actually been waffling about it, and what had happened during his tour of the premises had left him seriously wavering. But finding out about the Manaar gig tipped the scales, and tipped them good and hard: there was no way in hell he was missing this show. Besides, al-Wahid had made it pretty clear that he wanted everyone who'd played the last tour.

The sleet had eased up by the time the Mancusos were ready to head off, but it hadn't stopped. Bree and I had bundled up in our cold weather gear, and gone out to their car with them.

"Jesus, Bree, are you crazy, coming outside if you don't have to?" Katia, wrapped in a huge quilted coat, looked cold just thinking about it. "It's about ten degrees out there and breathing in is like sucking on a popsicle the size of a baseball bat. You're going to freeze to death. Are you trying to get sick? Like having to get this thing together in seven weeks isn't going to be crazy enough even if everyone's healthy?"

"It'll be fine." Bree'd wrapped herself in her cashmere coat, and was slipping on a pair of gloves and a hat. "John has this cool new coat. It's got a lightweight zip-out lining that feels like you're wrapping yourself in a down comforter, except that it doesn't bulk him up like a bear. It's the perfect coat for a horrible winter." She shivered. "And it isn't even winter yet, technically. Brrr."

"Bree's right, this thing's brilliant. Leather jackets don't keep the cold out, not the way they used to. But yeah, we're coming outside—not sure we're going to get much chance for talking for the next little while. Depends on what you decide to do." I moved the curtain aside. "Looks like your car's here."

We didn't actually say much, after all. I watched Tony climb in; round the other side of the car, Katia was already clicking her safety belt. I heard Bree's voice, a low murmur: *Remember, we're right here, call any time, I don't care when or why, I'm right here if you need me,* and Katia, sounding really calm, especially for her: *I know. I will.*

43

They drove off, east towards Central London. Bree and I watched their tail lamps disappear round the corner, tiny ice crystals dancing about in the wind, and headed indoors, shedding the coats and the gloves.

"Crikey." I watched Bree get the gear up on pegs, so that the central heating could dry them out. Even five minutes out of doors had left things damp; her cashmere looked to have a layer of frost on the shoulders. "It's cold enough the freeze the bollocks off a brass monkey out there."

"It won't be in Manaar, will it? Arabia's warm, right? I suppose that's something to look forward to." She sounded deadpan, no way to tell what she was really thinking or feeling. "I think I want something hot to drink—what time is it? Oh good, plenty of time to have some cocoa or something and not have to get up five times during the night. This getting old thing sucks."

"Yeah, I know what you mean. But it's only half past nine. We should be fine. Did you say cocoa? I wouldn't say no to that. Have you got any of your sugar substitute, so that you can have some as well...?"

Nice after-dinner conversation, the sort of thing any couple might talk about as she did the washing-up and he dried things and put them back in their proper places. Bree scraped a vanilla bean and seethed it in milk, beat some bitter dark cocoa into it, added some sweetener, and poured us each a cup. Over the rim, she looked at me.

"John, you've got that look on your face. There's something you want to say, isn't there? What's wrong?"

"You've got good eyes, lady." I took a deep breath. "Nothing wrong, but yeah, I've got a straight question. And feel free to tell me it's none of my business, all right?"

"Katia doesn't know who Tony saw. He didn't tell her." She smiled, a faint smile but a real one. "Was that it?"

"Sorry, love. Yeah, that was the main thing. I'm actually glad about that. Asking you to keep that sort of secret would have been a bit much, even coming from your best friend. But there was something else. Are you really okay with the Manaar show? And don't look at the wall or the clock or your shoes, love, please. Because I get the feeling you're not okay with it, and you know what, Bree, you get a vote. The way you feel about it, that matters to me. Just, let me know now, all right? Not later."

"I'm fine with it." She wrinkled her nose suddenly. "Shit, okay, maybe *fine* is the wrong word. I'm not fine with it. I'd rather not have anything to do with that guy, and the idea of you having to be somewhere where people's hands end up in picnic coolers isn't the happiest thought in the world. But I think you should do it anyway, John. I really do."

"You sure, Bree?" I was watching her face, trying to see what was going on in there. What she was saying was upfront, it was straightforward enough; the problem was, I wasn't entirely sure I believed it. There was something else happening there, something she'd shuttered, something I couldn't quite sort out. "Because you don't look happy, and if you're not –"

"I'm sure." She tilted the mug suddenly, and drained it. *Shit.* She hadn't lost the old talent for hiding things, not entirely. "It's fine. I wonder where I can get a bathing suit in London in the middle of November? Or is Manaar one of those places where women are supposed to cover up everything...?"

Katia rang Bree the next afternoon, to let her know that Tony had checked into the Recovery Centre. The women went off to shop for warm weather gear together, which was just as well. I'd got a call from Ian rather earlier in the day than he'd usually ring, to let me know we had another sit-down meeting at Fallow House that afternoon, dinner would be provided, this was going to be the "here's the details and you lot have all got to vote on it" deal, and had I heard from Tony?

So I was able to tell him that, yeah, Tony was here but he was officially out of circulation for the next twenty nine days, non-negotiable. I let Ian know that Tony wanted to do the Manaar gig, and Katia would probably be happy to come along to the meeting to hammer out details on Tony's behalf, if Ian needed that to happen. Of course, Ian had dealt with Katia handling Tony's stuff for him before; she's like a laser beam when it comes to his finances, and if you fuck with her, she can get just as scary as Domitra. So I wasn't surprised when Ian told me no, not at this point in the proceedings. Just before we rang off, he cleared his throat.

"JP, half a tick, please. There's something I need to ask you, and I don't want to do it in front of the band. Fuck, I don't want to ask it at all." I could practically hear him bracing himself. "Look, you know Tony better than any of us. And you've been down this road yourself. So I need to know. You think he'll be ready? Clean enough to handle it?"

For a moment, I felt myself stiffen up. Stupid, really, that reaction was: Ian wasn't trying to insult anyone, he was doing his job. It was a fair question, considering how much money was on the table here...

"JP? Sorry." He sounded worried. "Look, not trying to offend you, but I've got to ask."

"No, I know. I really do get it, Ian, and yeah, you do have to ask. Short answer? He could probably do it tomorrow. He's been dry for a few weeks now, and sticking to it, and yeah, I'm sure. Like you said, I've been down that road. But he needs time and space to sort it out and get it together. Rushing him won't do any good. We've got seven weeks. Barring something no one can control, Act of God or whatever, he'll be ready."

"Good." Back to being basic Ian Hendry. "That's one thing off my list of shit to worry about, then. See you in about an hour. I'm sending a car for Mac. Do you want your own driver, or should I tell him to come get you as well? And is Bree coming along today...?"

46

That first meeting had been short and not too tricky, mostly because the rest of us had been busy gawking after the small tactical nuke Mac and Luke had dropped on our heads. This time, with the proposal on the table and some hard information to kick about, things were a lot more complicated.

For one thing, everyone showed up without their old ladies. Of course Dom was there—if Mac's someplace, so is she—but she was the only band woman on the premises. That set the tone early on. Like it or not, when the band wives are there, the vibe is different, and so is the language.

I could tell the moment I walked through the front door at Fallow House that Ian was twitchy, wanting to get down to business. He's not an idiot, though; we got fed first, and warmed up, and then the two blokes who make up the night janitorial staff cleared everything away except the pile of paper in front of Ian.

"All right." Ian wasn't wasting time or breath, and that by itself was enough to clue me in to how big a deal this gig was. He'd booked us for the Superbowl Halftime Show and hadn't looked as piano-wire taut as he did right then. He jerked his head towards the phone on the sideboard. It's got a video hook-up, but they'd been left off. "Carla? Patrick? Roll call."

"We're both here." Carla sounded her usual self. "Patrick was actually finishing up a case and his client was in Glendale, so he just came here for this instead of heading north to San Francisco. Hi, guys."

"Brilliant." Ian was back looking at us. "Here's the basics, and do me a favour, will you, don't say a word until I'm done. After that, I'm going to want all the input I can get. All right?"

Silence. Ian's done that before, but not at the beginning of one of these things—it's usually after we start shouting at each other, trying to give us all a time-out. This was a new twist for him.

I looked sideways at Luke, who'd pulled up a chair and parked

47

himself next to me. His eyebrows were a nice deep vee. Whatever Ian had, Luke didn't have the details.

"This arrived this morning, by diplomatic special courier. We've got a formal offer, a contract, a series of riders, a date, and the tech specs. The offer is just what Mac proposed: twelve million pounds for one show, New Year's Eve, to be held on some sort of municipal open grounds in the Emirate's capital city. Once the contract's signed and the rider details sorted out, there'd be a cheque for ten million pounds made out to Luke's non-profit, and a cheque for two million to the Kinkaid Recovery Centre. The braintrust for the resort would liaise with our people to make sure we've got everything we need, soup to nuts, tech to reservations. Carla, you and Ronan and Nial would be the ones doing most of the dealing on that. Security would be our baby, with cooperation from the palace, so there's Patrick and Dom with some major coordinating to do."

He stopped. Right. He'd asked for silence, and he was getting it. He tapped the papers in front of him.

"One more thing, and we're off. The projected audience figure is a quarter-million people."

Yeah, well, so much for the babble and blather he'd expected. You could have heard a fly die, the silence was that absolute.

Cal Wilson got his voice back first. "Um—yeah, okay. Leaving aside the question of just why that nutter al-Wahid is so desperate to get us out there to play, I want to make sure I heard you right. Did you say something about 'open grounds'? Can you clarify that? Because that doesn't sound as if there's a venue in place. Where would we be staging a gig for a quarter million people, in the middle of the local park? Or maybe on a sand dune?"

"It might as well be the local park, from the looks of it, apart from it being huge." Ian slid a stack loose from the pile. "Fuck, I'm an idiot. I meant to pass these round—here, there's copies for everyone. Carla, you have the one I faxed? Good. The site photos were taken just a couple of days ago, so this is the current gen. They're at the bottom of the stack. You tell me. Is this doable, or should I tell him to take his twenty four million quid and sod off? Nial? Ronan?"

"Oh, it's doable." Nial didn't quite shrug. "Since we won't have a handle on the physical layout and whatnot until we get out there, I'd want a really stripped-down design for this, something literally straight from the can. A call to Tait Towers would do it—I'd have them send over whatever they've got as the current flavour of basic stadium end stage. Ronan?"

"Yeah, straight front of stage line arrays, a handful of remote towers, extra generators, bob's your uncle. Nothing like Book of Days—even if we fancied it, there's not enough time. I'm with Nial: let's keep it simple."

Of course, right then, it was a done deal. Ian let the conversations bounce about for a few minutes; from the looks of it, it was business as usual, him taking mental notes on what we wanted and the best way to get it done, and right round the time he'd sorted all that out in his head, he brought us back to it.

"Right. An official yea or nay vote's probably just a formality at this point, but before we do it, oi, Patrick! You and Dom have been quiet. What about the security for this do? You okay with this, or what?"

"Dom, ladies first? No? Okay." Patrick Ormand sounded just the way he always sounds. Hard to know what he's thinking—he's a former DEA bloke and homicide cop, and he does poker voice as well as he does poker face. The only time you ever get a real shift in there is if he thinks something or someone is bleeding upwind. "Personally, I'd like a few things added to our end of the rider. I'm looking at the stuff you faxed Carla, and I'd want a really delineated backstage area. Not only that, but considering who's hosting this shindig—not to mention paying for it—I'd want absolute control of the band areas, and that includes the hotel. I don't want any incidents with these people. One picnic basket of body parts was plenty for me. Dom? Did you say something?"

"Just rolling my eyes and snorting, that's all." She was, too. It takes something special to knock Domitra Calley off her balance. "I agree with Patrick. Need to know who handles what, right down to the molecules, yo. Band and security, we handle all of it. No one gets in or out of the designated band areas without our say-so. The rest of it, how should I know? I don't vote. That shit, that's up to my boss."

"Dom, what a peculiar thing to call me, especially when we both know perfectly well you could fold, spindle and mutilate me before I got enough air in my lungs to ask you what I'd done to piss you off." Mac peered around Luke and caught my eye. "I think we're ready for that vote, but can we clear up the question of Tony's availability? I hate to sound intrusive, but this is band business and after all, Ali specifically wants the Book of Days lineup for this. Johnny?"

"Tony's in. I've already hashed this out with him—he's sequestered, no outside contact, for four weeks starting this morning, then a week of couples counselling with Katia. He'll be done with the Recovery Centre in five weeks, the gig's in seven. He told me to tell you he wouldn't miss it."

"Good." Ian stood up. "You lot know the drill. Hands up if you think Blacklight ought to do it. Crikey, not a single nay vote? Right, then, makes my job easier. I'll get hold of al-Wahid's people in the morning, and we'll have drafts of our own riders done by end of business tomorrow. Meanwhile, I'd ask that you please read what they sent us. Read it really carefully and yes, Mac, I mean you especially. You know him, we don't. If there's anything in that pile that twigs you wrong, let me know. We'll talk about rehearsals tomorrow."

Chapter Four

"(beep)…JP? It's Ian. Look, I hate to do this to you, but we need to do a fast run out to Manaar, and have a sit-down with al-Wahid and his people. Patrick wants a look at the security issues before he starts hiring staff, and we really ought to get a feel for the site before the gear arrives from Tait. No need to drag Bree along if she'd rather stay in London, this is really just band personnel signing off on a few things. Carla's got a private plane reserved for us out of Heathrow. She's flying out tonight, and Patrick flew out this morning. They'll meet us there. I'll have a car at your place tomorrow morning at half past ten. Sorry it's that early, but it's a seven-hour flight and a four-hour time difference. Be ready to go, will you? Call me if you've got questions. (beep)"

"Oh bloody hell!"

"Uh-oh." Bree was busy kneading dough—she'd said something about wanting a decent loaf of egg bread—but she turned round at that. "That doesn't sound good. What's wrong?"

"I'm being dragged off to fucking Manaar tomorrow, is what." The look on her face got me hurrying into an explanation. "Not to worry, Ian says you don't have to go. He just needs the band to sign off on some things. It's just the band."

"Oh, shit." She sat down, hard. "*Shit!*"

I blinked at her. "Bree, what? I know it's a drag, but I'll only be gone a couple of days."

"Did you say the band needs to sign things?" She sounded resigned. "Doesn't that mean Tony? Because he can't, can he? Katia's his designated representative."

I opened my mouth, and shut it again. I'd got the reason for her swearing now, good and clear.

If anything needs band signatures, it means the entire band has to agree. That's Blacklight's policy, ironclad, the way we've always done things. As a hard policy, it's worked for us from the beginning, and we've never seen any reason to change it. And for this gig, of all gigs, it was vital. I reached for my phone.

"Right. I'm ringing Ian, make sure he's thought about that. Wait, is that yours ringing?"

It was Katia, and listening to Bree's end of the conversation, I put my phone down again. Ian had thought of it, all right. From the pitch of Katia's voice at the other end of the phone, she was right at the edge of flipping her shit.

"No." Bree's shoulders were mauls of tensed muscle, but Katia wouldn't know that. It floored me, that she could look so tense and sound so Zen. "That's silly. You're not deserting Tony if you go to Manaar, you're helping him. What? No! Katia, would you please take a breath? No, I am not being condescending and I'm not talking down to you, either. I just don't think you're thinking this through all the way. He can't go anywhere himself and anyway, it's not like you can visit him or any-

52

thing, right? You'd be acting as his agent, so why are you freaking out?"

Katia's voice crackled through the phone, higher pitched than usual. I knew what was being said—it was obvious from Bree's face, and of course, we'd both seen it coming. It was about the last thing in the world she wanted to do, but she'd made a promise to be there for Katia. And Bree doesn't break promises.

"Of course I'll come too, if you want me there." Nice calm voice, eyes as bleak as the weather outside. "Look, let me get off the phone so that John can let Ian know. Try and get some sleep. We'll see you at the airport tomorrow morning."

She clicked off. Before she could put the phone down, or smash it against the wall, I was up and across the kitchen, with both arms wrapped round her tight, talking into her hair. She was rigid as a wrought iron railing.

"You know what, love, you're a good friend. Best friend Katia could have, now or ever. It'll be all right. It'll be two days at the most, nice private plane, a break from this crap weather, and back again. We're not hanging out there for fun, just business and back. Bree? Gordon *Bennett*, are you crying? Love, what is it? What's wrong?"

"I'm sorry." She pulled back, just enough to get a hand free and dash tears off her face. "I'm being a total pill. I just—I don't want to go, I don't want you to go, I don't want Katia to go. The idea of having to go be polite to that man makes my skin crawl. I just hate the idea and yes, I know I said I think you should do the show and I meant it, John, I swear I did, but I really need to figure out how to deal with this."

I know my wife. I understand that she gets wound up, sometimes about stuff I wouldn't think twice about. Sometimes she's dead right, seeing things about a situation that I've missed. But this was about as extreme as I'd ever seen from Bree.

So I held on and stayed quiet. It didn't seem a moment for

pushing it, and I wouldn't have known where to push anyway. If she was really sorting it out in her head, the best thing I could do was shut my gob and wait. Pushing wasn't going to get much done beyond muddying up what she was trying to get clear.

"It's on his turf." She was speaking slowly. She'd pulled back from me, not withdrawing, just enough so that I could see her face. "When we saw him before, dealt with him before, it was on our turf. We had home court. Mac apologised to me for that, for inviting that man to my house without clearing it with me first, but he did the right thing and I told him so, John. It was absolutely the right move. Ali al-Wahid really didn't like having to cope with that situation somewhere where he wasn't in control, did he? He hated having to apologise at all, but he really hated having to do it on our turf, where he had no control. He's used to having control."

"Yeah, he did." I was remembering that encounter, and Bree was right—it had been there in the way al-Wahid had changed colour, the way he'd tightened up. "He really didn't fancy being surrounded, either. That's what's freaking you out about this, Bree? That we have to go there, because us being there means he gets to call the tune?"

"It's part of it, anyway." Her eyes were clouded. "I just keep remembering that he has more money and power than anyone has any business having, and that he's not too careful about what he does with either thing. Either that, or he's a fucking idiot, and that makes him pretty damned scary. I mean, Jesus, John, he hired a pair of traditional Moslems to watch his twin tramps. Would anyone with half a brain do that?"

"Damned if I know." She was right, dead right. If he'd been that arrogant in our parlour, half a world away from the safety of his own ground, how bad was he likely to be while he was sitting in his favourite armchair or throne or whatever, in his own palace overlooking his private bit of oceanfront property? *Shit.* "But it's not so much about his brains, is it? It's his judgement that's the problem. I'm not convinced this little face to face is going to be that bad, Bree. For one thing, I don't care how many harem guards or eunuchs with swords or dancing girls he's got at his back, we've got the whip hand."

She blinked at me. "We do?"

"Hell yeah. Strength in numbers, love. All it would take is one of us getting pissed off enough to say right, that's rubbish and I'm not playing the show, and the rest of the band would walk. And yeah, that goes for Katia saying it, as well. She's standing in for Tony, and her vote is his vote. And there's something else, Bree. I've no clue why he wants us to do this, but he does, enough to pay out all that dosh. That gives us damned near all the power. We can deny him what he wants, you know? We don't even have to know what it is."

She was quiet, watching my face. I bent a knuckle and chucked her under the chin; that's a gesture I use a lot less often than I used to, when we were both younger. This time, it surprised her enough to get a smile out of her.

"No worries, Bree, all right? We don't owe Ali al-Wahid a damned thing, and however it goes down, I'm not taking any shit from him or anyone else."

I'd been half-expecting some drama from Katia on the flight to Manaar, but in the end there was nothing, and thank God for it. She'd pulled Bree aside for a fast conversation that looked to be pretty much to the point, even though it was all done in whispers. Bree listened and nodded, and then she stepped out of the way because there was Ian, taking Katia under his wing, settling in next to her on the plane, clueing her in. No idea what he told her, but whatever it was, it did the trick. When the pilot set us down at al-Wahid's private airstrip, Katia was herself again: not calm, because calm isn't her thing, but level-headed and ready to deal on Tony's behalf.

That was a load off Bree's mind, I could tell. She'd finished that *tete à tete* with Katia all tensed up, but Ian moving in and taking over, that took care of it. It took so much weight off my wife's shoulders, she actually dozed off in the seat next to me for the last two hours of the flight.

Yeah, well, that didn't last. The plane's engines hadn't throttled all the way down before, and Bree'd woken up and was stretching, when the pilot's voice came over the speakers.

"Ladies and gentlemen, I've been asked to tell you that there will be a short delay in getting you off the plane." He sounded nervous. "The Emir has a personal envoy en route to greet you. Apparently the official limousines were a little late leaving the Palace, but they'll be here shortly. They've—requested that everyone stay on board until then. Thanks for your understanding and patience."

Oh, bloody hell.

Next to me, Bree was stiff. Envoy from the Palace, yeah, right. *Shit.* If Ali al-Wahid was trying to remind us that we were on his turf now, and had to play by his rules, he'd made a brilliant job of it. I hadn't missed that nervous little hesitation in the pilot's voice, before he'd said the word "request", and what's more, neither had my wife. Bree went from sleepy to stone-faced in about ten seconds.

Request, my arse. That was an order, a display of power, and no argy-bargy about it, either. We hadn't even got off the plane yet and this trip was already completely fucked.

We only had about ten minutes wait before we heard the portable stairs being rolled up to the door at the front of the plane. It might as well have been a year. Bree and I weren't the only ones reacting badly to al-Wahid's heavy-handed rubbish; that ten minutes had been completely silent. Even with no one saying a word, though, there was no way you could miss how pissed off everyone was. The silence in the cabin was so thick, the damned plane felt as if it were seething.

Right around the time the pilot came back on to tell us the doors were opening, welcome to the Royal Emirate of Manaar and he'd hoped we'd all had a nice comfy flight, Mac got up, and Domitra with him. He'd been at school with al-Wahid, so maybe he had a better clue about what the protocol was supposed to be. More likely, he'd just got bored with sitting about, or with the idea of humouring his old school chum. Personally, I didn't give a toss what this particular lot wanted us to do. What I'd told Bree was true: if one of us decided to say *sod it, not playing this gig* and walk, we all would. Just then, I was narked almost to the point of saddling whoever the envoy was with the job of telling his boss or master or whatever *right, fuck off then, I'm not playing, the gig's off*…

"Ladies and gentlemen, the stairs are in place and the representative from the Palace is ready for the official greeting." The pilot sounded seriously shaken up. Made me wonder how often he'd done this run, London to Manaar, and what they'd threatened him with if he cocked it up. "Your cars are waiting. If everyone is ready to disembark…?"

Bree and I were second down the steps, right behind Mac and Dom. Bree was in front of me—ladies first, yeah?—which is why, when she stopped dead halfway down, I nearly broke both of our necks running into her. She said something under her breath, but I couldn't quite make it out. Behind me, Luke said something a lot easier to understand. He hadn't brought Karen with him, which was just as well; she blushes easily, for a redhead.

Our cars were there, all right, four bullet-proof jobs. There were liveried drivers standing next to each limo, doing that whole "stare at nothing and don't blink" thing they do, as part of the gig. Our escort was there, as well.

It was Almanzor al-Wahid. The Emir had come himself.

"Malcolm." He made straight for Mac. He wasn't waiting to see what anyone else was going to do. Explained why the pilot had sounded so twitchy, yeah? "I am pleased to see you all. I had intended to send staff, but it seemed best to greet you myself. I hope your flight was a good one?"

I opened my mouth, and shut it again, swallowing the words that wanted out: *oh please, mate, you don't give one single damn what the flight was like, or about anything else, either.* Yeah, it was his turf, his rules, all right. He wasn't saying or doing anything we could actually object to, but it was there in the tone of his voice, the set of his shoulders. He just stood there, face smooth and unreadable, completely in control.

I suddenly remembered him standing in our front room at 2828 Clay Street. His face hadn't stayed smooth that day, because Luke had verbally taken him to pieces, peeling long bleeding strips off al-Wahid's ego.

That wasn't happening today. If I'd needed a clear example of why Bree wanted this sort of encounter on her own home ground, this was it.

"The flight was fine, thanks." Mac had hit the tarmac, with Dom at his side. I'm quite familiar with her body language, the way she moves in particular situations. This was an interesting moment: she was watchful, but she wasn't on high alert. That meant she was ready to kill someone if they needed it, but she wasn't seeing the need, at least not yet. It also meant she wasn't actively expecting it.

The luggage was being unloaded from the plane, and into an SUV with blacked-out windows. Mac was looking around, at our luggage from the looks of it, making sure it got into the truck. What he wasn't doing was offering a hand for his old school friend to shake. That was peculiar, considering how formal this whole set-up was. I watched the Emir look at Mac's hands, watched his eyebrows go up, and I suddenly got it: Mac knew there was a game to be played, and he was on it.

Right. If our frontman was going to handle Ali al-Wahid and

his tree-pissing bullshit, I could relax and give my attention where it was needed, which was making sure nothing happened that triggered Bree into any kind of meltdown.

I got a hand in the small of her back. She was wearing a light shirt; we'd checked the weather for Manaar before we'd left London, and she'd changed into something that worked better for the 80-plus degrees Fahrenheit Manaar was enjoying than what she'd had on in London.

The small of her back is where she keeps her moods. I can always tell how she's doing by getting the palm of my hand right there, and just then, it was flaming hot. *Shit.* Not good. I was damned if I was having her made nuts, not by Ali al-Wahid or anyone else.

"Can we move on, love? We've got a queue behind us."

She glanced at me over her shoulder. Whatever she saw in my face, it did the trick; I watched the tension go out of her upper body. She went down the ramp and stood off to one side, looking past my shoulder at Ian and Katia.

Even in December, the temperature was too warm for my taste. I had a moment of thinking that, if all of Arabia was this hot, it must have taken some kind of sadist to have dreamed up all those veils and layers they seem to want their women to use as gear. Of course, coming from not quite freezing and a sky full of sleet back in London, it probably felt hotter than it actually was.

"When you are all ready? Your bags are secured." The Emir had gone back to being smooth and unreadable. Sod it. Not my problem, whatever the game was between him and Mac.

But he wasn't watching Mac, not anymore. He'd moved on to Luke. I don't know if he expected Luke to do something, or say something, but if he did, it wasn't on. Luke nodded at him, and looked over his head. Luke's over six feet, and al-Wahid was my height. Home turf isn't the only advantage out there, you know?

"Good, the limos are here. I hope they're air-conditioned." Ian had hit the ground with Katia at his heels, and unlike Mac, he held out a hand to shake. He sounded as gruff as he usually does, and he wasn't bothering about any protocol rubbish, but I thought al-Wahid looked relieved that someone wasn't actually snubbing him on his own airstrip, for a change. "Any sign of Patrick and Carla? Because they're the reason we're here, and we're not really scheduled to let this visit go long."

"Your head of security and operations manager are already here. They arrived this morning, and are my honoured guests at the Queen's Palace, as you all will be." He gave Katia a smile, pleasant enough. "If you are ready...?"

The liveried drivers were all at full attention. It was rather like watching some sort of Christmas display in the windows of the Regent Street shops, except in pantomime: they looked like clockwork soldiers, windup toys all moving together. I saw something move across Bree's face, distaste maybe, or just being uncomfortable with all of it, wanting to get the hell out of it and go home. I got one arm round her waist, and turned us towards the nearest limo.

"Here we go," I told her. "Let's get out of the heat, all right? Sun's giving me a spiker of a headache."

We climbed in, Bree going ahead of me. The limos looked to be designed for no more than four, and Cal and Stu had already climbed in. The driver shut the door behind us, and a moment later, we'd pulled off and away into traffic, past shiny steel skyscrapers glinting under a hard sun at the edge of the water, heading off towards Manaar's royal compound.

I had hold of Bree's hand, not talking, letting Stu and Cal natter. I wasn't telling her that, as she'd got settled in, I'd got a nice clear look through the window, at our host.

He hadn't been watching Mac, or Luke, not anymore. He hadn't been keeping an eye on his own people, either. He'd been staring in through the window of our limo, and his eyes had been fixed firmly on my wife.

I hadn't really given any thought to what our digs in Manaar were likely to be like. I mean, right, I'd expected comfort and probably luxury; for whatever reason, he seemed to be sucking up to us as a band in a big way, and he didn't strike me as the sort of bloke to deny himself anything he fancied. And yeah, I'd heard him say something about Carla and Patrick being put up at some queen's palace. But I'd been too busy trying to sort out why our host had been looking at my wife as if she was something he'd need to call in military manoeuvres to cope with to wonder about where we were going to be sleeping tonight.

Still, he was all about luxury, and not doing anything on the cheap. So when the limos pulled into the compound, and we got our first look at the Queen's Palace, I probably shouldn't have been quite as floored as I was.

"Bloody hell, is he joking!" Stu, peering out the window, snorted. I couldn't tell if he was snorting at the design of the thing, or at how over the top it was. There were peacocks and hens wandering about, giving the limos dirty looks. "We sleeping in a fucking *seraglio*, or something? We get regulation folding cots in this bloke's harem?"

It was nuts. We drove through a set of arches that would have put the gates at Buckingham Palace to shame; they reminded me vaguely of something, I couldn't quite sort out what, but after a minute, I realised I'd been thinking of the Taj Mahal: similar shape, a lot more colour. The gates were the same blue as all those peacock tails out front, and they were trimmed in what was probably liquid gold. Nothing would have surprised me at that point. It wasn't until later that I sussed out that the liquid gold paint had been used in a way to make the patterns on the gates look as if they'd had those peacock tails posed in place.

61

Inside, we pulled to a stop in a courtyard. The liveried driver got out and opened the door for us. Bree was first out, and just as she reached for the driver's hand, to help her out, the bloke was brushed away as if he were a gnat or something.

"Please allow me. I claim a host's privilege."

al-Wahid was smiling at Bree, one hand held out. There was no way for her to refuse, not without a level of rudeness that was probably beyond her. I know fuck-all about protocol or any of that rubbish, but there was something about this place that felt formal, and ancient, as if they took this stuff really seriously and had been doing it for a really long time, as well. And it was his limo, his courtyard, his turf.

Poor Bree was stuck, and she knew it. She glanced back at me, and I felt our usual line of marital thought-reading kick in hard: *I know, but we're guests.*

And she got it. She turned back again, and let the Emir get hold of one of her hands, and help her out.

"Thank you." Her voice was completely neutral, and so was her face. She's usually rotten when it comes to hiding things, but just then, she must have felt a major need, because even I was having trouble sussing out what she was feeling. "That's very kind of you. John…?"

"Right here, love." I was already out, no help offered by the owner of all this luxury. Something in me was kicking hard against that whole formality thing. "Nice digs you've got here, mate. Queen's Palace, you said? Didn't know there was a queen. She all right with us parking our bags in her sauna, then?"

I heard a snort from behind me. The other limos had pulled up and emptied out, and Mac had come up, Domitra glued to his side. Mac was just Mac—not sure if he'd ever been tense in the first place. Dom, though, she hadn't relaxed.

"There is no queen, not today." al-Wahid was matching my wife in being inscrutable, but he was looking straight at Bree again. It

62

was very weird—he wasn't being gallant, and he wasn't attracted either. Trust me, I know when a bloke's hitting on my wife. But she wasn't the only woman there, and he was basically ignoring Katia and Dom. "The queen for whom this was built was my great-grandmother. She has been dead these many years, but she would not begrudge its use in any case. She is legendary among my people for her love of music, and musicians. My people will bring your belongings to your quarters—Ms. Fanucci and Mr. Ormand are resting, but will join us for dinner, at my personal table. I would be honoured to show you more of the Palace, if you will allow me…?"

Next to me, I saw Mac's lips purse up in a whistle. Not stupid, Ali al-Wahid. He was still talking directly to my wife but he wasn't offering a hand, or talking down to her. She wasn't unbending at all, but she shot me a fast look. This one was dead easy to read: *what the hell is this guy's trip…?*

I shrugged back at her: *no clue.* It was true. I couldn't sort out why he was taking so much trouble over Bree. She had no power to sign anything, she wasn't playing the gig, and she was here as the ornament on the man's arm, a band wife in a culture where wives aren't valued much to begin with, except as property or producers of little boys. I couldn't make sense of any of it.

Meanwhile, al-Wahid was giving us a sort of spoken Grand Tour, talking about his grandmother's digs. He waved an arm towards a series of pools that looked like something you might see in a Vegas hotel on the strip, or maybe that was the wrong way round. There were nine of them, nice and big.

"These pools are for the use of my guests—they are heated by the natural hot springs beneath Manaar. The minerals in the water are considered very healthy. My great-grandmother lived into her nineties. They are for your private use. I believe you drive a Jaguar, Mrs. Kinkaid. Is that not correct?"

We all stopped, just blinking at him. The question was so unexpected, it surprised Bree into an honest response.

"How the hell did you know that?" She blurted it out. "And what does my car have to do with anything?"

"Only that, if you wish, I am happy to put any of my cars at your disposal." One point to the Emir; he'd scored, and he knew it. "If you have a love of speed, perhaps my Bugatti would please you? Our roads are straight and uncluttered, and can be closed to other traffic should you choose. Let me know if this would suit you. Ah, here is the Queen's Kitchen. It has been made rather more modern than my great-grandmother would have recognised, but as you can see, it is not yet ready for full use; there is still work to be done. Our chef in residence is Paris trained…"

I missed most of the history lesson he dragged us through, because my brain was elsewhere, trying to suss out what he was up to with Bree. He wasn't flirting, and it wasn't a come-on, either. She had no power in this situation, none at all; Christ, that was why she hadn't wanted to come in the first place, knowing she was going to feel powerless on his turf.

I glanced over at Mac. Any hope that he might know what was going on went out the window; he was looking at his old school chum as if he'd only just met him.

We followed al-Wahid through arches, down between the hot mineral pools. I wasn't paying much attention to the tour guide thing he was doing, but I did notice that all the windows were high up in the walls, and very small. They also all had grilles over them, and a thought popped into my head: *I wonder if his great-grandmother was trying to keep people in, or keep people out?*

Eventually, either al-Wahid got tired of showing off the columns and pools, or else he'd run out of things to show off, because he finally led us through the one set of arches we hadn't been through, and into a corridor that was shaded, and dark, and looked to be made of limestone or marble or something. There was also a series of proper doors. Turned out the doors had proper rooms behind them.

"Forgive me. I take so much pride in sharing my home, I forget my manners. I am sure you wish to rest. You are my honoured guests at dinner tonight. I will send equerries to escort you. This section of the Palace is entirely at your disposal for as long as you are here—each suite has the name of its guest on the door. I ask you to forgive the simplicity of these accommodations, but the suites I commissioned are not yet completed. When you are next here, there will be comfort at a higher level."

He nodded at Dom, gave Katia a smile of sorts, bowed over Bree's hand again, and left. We stood there, the lot of us, totally silent, listening to his footsteps die away. From outside, I could hear birds singing, and the water in the pools bubbling away.

"He's right about one thing. I could use a nice nap." Mac's eyebrows were up, and he sounded as bemused as I've ever heard him. "Bree, angel, if you don't mind my asking, what in sweet hell was all that about? Why was Ali sucking up to you? And yes, in case you were wondering, that was a complete and thorough suck-up. He offered to let you drive his pretty shiny Veyron, and that bloody car cost over a million quid. What in hell?"

"Shit, he offered to close down the motorway." Dom was watching Bree as well. They all were. "He in love, or what? What's up with Ali Baba offering you the keys to the kingdom and the keys to the car, yo?"

"You tell me and we'll both know." There was trouble in Bree's face. "I don't get it. It's not like I have anything he wants, or anything I would be willing to give him if I did. I don't know. And right now, I think I want to take my shoes off and lock the door and lie down for awhile, because I am so damned creeped out, you can't begin to imagine. I hope there are real beds in there, and not just stupid floor cushions and bowls for peeled grapes. John? Please tell me one of those doors has our name on it...?"

If the rooms were anything to go by, the eastern notion of sim-

65

plicity is rather different from mine. Turned out the Hotel Harem, or whatever al-Wahid was actually calling his granny's blue and gold pleasure palace these days, not only had proper doors, it had proper locks on them and hot Jacuzzi tubs in the bath, as well.

That was just as well, because my wife was frazzled as hell. She was so freaked, she was actually mumbling to herself. I could hear her while I was getting the water in the tub good and warm, and dumping in some of the fancy salts from the bottles on the edge of the tub. The room was actually on the cool side. No idea if it was the thick stone walls keeping the heat of the sun out, or whether it was really effective air conditioning, and I didn't give a toss, not just then.

"...his Bugatti?" She'd shed everything she was wearing and headed straight for the tub. "I don't even know how to drive a manual. John? Why would he offer me his Bugatti?"

"Bree, I don't even know what a Bugatti is. Here, you get in before that water cools down too much to do you any good."

"It's a car. A very pretty, very expensive car. It's the fastest car in the world. Does he think I'm Michael Schumacher? Do I *look* like Michael Schumacher?" She slid all the way down. The water was up round her chin. "What the hell is going on? John?"

"I don't know who Michael Schumacher is, either. I'm betting he doesn't look half as good as you do, though. Especially without his clothes on, yeah?"

I turned the Jacuzzi on, and parked myself on the edge of the tub. No idea what it was made of, but it looked like marble. I could feel the chill of the stone, straight through my trousers. "Bloody hell, that's got better bubbles than your favourite champagne! Bree, look, I've got a suggestion. Why don't we just skip all the imperial intrigue rubbish, and ask the bloke what he thinks he's on about? Want me to have a go?"

She'd settled down in the tub and closed her eyes, but they

popped open at that. "Wow. Would you really do that? Just go ask him, I mean?"

"Fuck yeah. Why wouldn't I? The bloke may think he's in some Hollywood flick about Lorenzo de Medici or Lawrence of Arabia or something, but that doesn't mean we've got to go along with it." I got up. "You have a nice hot soak. I'm off to find out why Sheikh Moneybags is sucking up to my wife."

Of course I got lost.

I suppose it wasn't surprising. I hadn't really been paying attention, back in the limo, coming in under those huge blue and gold arches; I'd been too busy gawking at the arches themselves. So I hadn't noticed that the road we'd come in on wasn't the only one in. There were five more just like it.

I stopped a minute, trying to orient myself. Right. Had those pools been off to my right? No way to tell; from the looks of it, the place was a quadrangle. I suddenly had a picture in my head: walking down the corridor at the recovery centre in London, scoping it out for Tony. There'd been a gardener out there in the sleety downpour, deadheading roses and looking miserable.

I looked up and around. The place was bloody confusing, and I was getting overheated too quickly for comfort. The MS doesn't like extremes in weather, you know? It's not wild about stress or time zone changes, either. And yeah, there were probably half a million people shivering back in the UK right now who'd have swapped places with me in a heartbeat, but the fact is, standing about in one place triggers ataxia in both legs. Doing it with eighty degrees of sun beating down on my head, in a disused harem too close to the equator for my comfort levels, just made it worse. And I'm not much for palm trees, anyway.

I shook my head, and sweat ran down into my eyes. It stung, and I lifted a hand to wipe it away. The hand was shaking, a sharp nasty little tremor. So were both legs.

Right, Johnny. Time to get the hell out of it. Just pick an arch with a road and see if it leads to Almanzor al-Wahid. Just pick a direction, and go there.

I took a step forward. A vicious little jolt of myokimia ran straight up from my left ankle to my hip, and both legs went out from under me.

It wasn't a bad fall, but it was a fall. I went down on both knees; in that situation, most people put a hand out to try easing the impact, but I'm a guitar player and I've trained myself not to do that. I need my hands. So I let my knees take the hit. They didn't enjoy it much.

"Shit!"

Weird acoustics the place had; I heard my own voice echoing round the courtyard, *shit shit shit*. It was still echoing when I heard a splash, definitely the sound of water moving in one of the pools behind me, off to one side, and the slap of bare feet on the tiles.

I took a breath, and started up off the ground. Not very dignified, but fuck, false pride about the MS does me sod all in the way of good. Having someone help me back to our room was worth having had someone watch me take a header. At least I hadn't done a faceplant; a state dinner with two black eyes would have just about put the tin cupola on what was shaping up to be a visit I was already planning on forgetting as soon as I feasibly could.

There was a hand under my left elbow, and another one under my right. Not much help, really, just sort of holding me while I pushed myself up. Small hands, they were, and very soft.

"Thanks." I was on my feet now, shaky but upright, brushing off the knees of my trousers. "Sorry about that. Can you tell me which way –"

Behind me, someone giggled. It was answered, call and response, just like two guitars echoing each other, by another voice, another giggle. I froze in place.

I'd heard this before, two little gigglers, fluttering and cooing. The tickybox in my chest was working overtime, kicking high and hard.

"Azra, he fell down! Should we call for a doctor?"

"But Paksima, if we do that, our father will know we were here. When he's angry, he's mean!" Her hand under my elbow tightened, ever so slightly. She was smiling, dark eyes nice and bold and very easy to read. "You're not so much hurt, are you?"

I looked down, left then right. They were both there, Ali al-Wahid's little blessings, his twin daughters, one on each side of me. The last time I'd seen these two, they'd been waving their arms, trying to seduce some poor roadie backstage at one of our shows, complete with their dimples and big dark eyes and modest spangled headscarves. Most of the roadies they'd managed to hook had ended up dead. They were bad news, those two.

The dimples and the eyes were present and accounted for, and all of it was being aimed straight at me. The scarves weren't, and neither was anything else in the way of actual clothing. One of the girls had a towel wrapped round her middle. The other one—I couldn't have told you which was which—was stark naked, shining with pool water.

"Right. Thanks. Cheers." *Right, Johnny, get the fuck out of here and don't waste any time about it, either. And whatever you do, don't touch either of them.*

I slipped between them, making damned sure I didn't so much as brush against either of them, back towards the safety of my nice chilly room and my nice warm wife. I didn't look behind me—I didn't need to. I knew just what they'd be up to: watching me, heads together, whispering.

Any conversation with their dad would have to wait.

Chapter Five

I'd thought the whole bit with Grandmother al-Wahid's soaking pools and peacocks and whatnot was decadent. But that was before I got dumped into the Emir's idea of a formal meal.

I don't know if the bloke ate his supper this way every night, or if he'd just had it laid on to impress the guests, or what. Either way, it was completely over the top. The only trick he missed was half-naked dancing girls feeding us figs, and he probably considered that. Mac said later he was surprised we hadn't been offered sheep's' eyes on a skewer by the pick of the local belly dancers. It was completely over the top.

Even with my own frustration at not having made it as far as al-Wahid's front parlour, I'd probably have enjoyed that dinner a lot more if both knees hadn't been making noise at me. It's always been a puzzle to me how you can fall, not tear the fabric of what you're wearing, and still come up with raw patches on the skin underneath. Doesn't matter how old I get, I don't fancy pain.

Back in the shaded corridor outside our room and safely out of the twins' line of sight, I'd actually hung out for a few minutes. I was waiting for my legs to stop shaking, but more to the point, my head was busy, coming up with rationales to convince myself it was all right to stay quiet about the twins: *Bree's already worried enough, the last thing she needs to hear is that the Persian Princesses are swanning round the seraglio naked just under our bedroom window, she'll flip her shit, no reason to give her more to worry about.*

It didn't take more than a minute to cop to the stupidity of that particular idea. Truth is, I gave Bree grief for years over her keeping things from me, the way she was making the pits we'd kept falling into with each other deeper and darker and dirtier by not being upfront with me. The last time one of us had kept a major secret, I'd been the one doing it. Her finding out about it—even though I'd had no choice—had nearly cost me my marriage.

So, right, not an option. I was going to have tell her.

I let myself back inside just as she was getting out of the bath. She was wrapping herself in a pricey-looking bath sheet; it reminded me, not very pleasantly, of the girls out there in the pool. "That was quick—John? Oh shit, babe, what?"

I told her what had just gone down: heat, ataxia, myokimia, naked and mostly-naked princesses, the lot. And of course, she ignored the Tahini Twins thing entirely. She was too busy using the house phone to demand that someone bring some stuff for my knees. You'd think I'd know my wife by now.

We got a nice comprehensive first aid kit delivered to our room within ten minutes. The bloke introduced himself: *Hello, my name is Nordine, I am your personal equerry for as long as you are the guests of Manaar, you have only to ask and all that.* Very nice manners, but I'm afraid Bree was a bit short with him. She just wanted to cope with my knees.

A few hours later, when he showed up to drive us to dinner, Bree apologised, and of course the bloke smiled politely and said something vague and waved it off. She was done up to the nines; I had both knees bandaged and was shakier than I liked under that particular set of circs. I'd had a short rest, but it hadn't helped much. Everything hurt like hell, legs, knees, even my back. There was an MS exacerbation just waiting to nail me. I could feel it ramping up.

I didn't fancy coping with dinner. I didn't fancy coping with Ali al-Wahid, or his horny giggling brats. All I really wanted was to get through a plate of something edible, get whatever band business that might come up taken care of, and head off to bed. Fortunately, I had serious backup on that one. When I get this messed up, Bree turns into a Valkyrie. She's especially fierce with the outside world.

"Hang on." She was sounding militant. Nordine had taken us under the arches and out along one of those gleaming white roads, towards a totally different pile of stone than the one we'd just come from. It was just as well I hadn't tried sorting out where to go before I'd fallen. "We're going to get some food and then we're getting the hell back to our room, and don't even think about arguing with me, John. Did you remember to pack some painkillers? I think I have a couple of TyCo with me."

"Not sure." It came out a bit slurred; as if the rest of it wasn't enough to have to cope with, trigeminal neuralgia was kicking in, creeping up along my jaw. *Shit.* I saw Bree's face tighten up, and tried to sound normal. "Doesn't matter. We can get something from the Emir."

"Like what? Opium? Morphine?" She sounded as tight as her own shoulders. I saw Nordine shoot her a look in the rear-view mirror. "Swell. I wouldn't trust a painkiller from this part of the world to be anything that wasn't designed to be shot straight into a vein. We're in Poppy Central, remember? That's how half these people got rich. The last thing you need is a bottle of highly addictive Silk Road pharmaceuticals. I think we've arrived. Whoa, is this actually someone's *house?*"

Nordine opened the door for Bree and stood off to one side, completely expressionless. I climbed out after her, and we just stood there, gawking.

I'm not sure what I'd been expecting. Something out of the Arabian Nights, probably, all marble and minarets and fancy gilded bits everywhere. Yeah, well, my mistake. The Emir had done a one-eighty. If he'd wanted an antidote to his Gran's peacocks and pools, he'd built himself the right house.

There were no mineral pools out in the front yard of this one, and no peacocks, either. This was four floors of exposed steel framework and gleaming white concrete that looked like something out of some futuristic sci-fi flick about New York. The windows looked to be taller than I was, but there was something about them, the dullness and lack of shine, that made me think they might be bullet-proof glass. We'd actually driven through security gates; they stretched off into the distance, and the damned things looked to be studded with laser triggers.

The Emir of Manaar's personal digs were about as modern as modern gets, and in completely the wrong way. The compound was about as unwelcoming as it was unappealing. Something about it was weirdly familiar, too. I couldn't quite pin it down, but whatever memory was being triggered at the back of my head, it wasn't good.

"Damn." Bree muttered it, under her breath. "It looks like a prison. Even without any bars on the windows, it looks like something you'd want to escape from. It's like bad science fiction or something. Horrible. Why would anyone want to live in that, if they didn't have to?"

"Damned if I know, but you nailed it. Place really does look like a prison. I could even tell you which one."

There it was, that memory: Herlong Prison, northeast edge of California. I'd spent a couple of hours there as a visitor, and even knowing I could walk out whenever I damned well wanted to, even with the warden being a huge Blacklight fan and going out of her way to make it tolerable, the only word I could find for the place was 'awful'.

My knees were throbbing, a sort of dull sting. So was my jaw. I reached out and got hold of Bree's hand.

"I'll tell you what, love, I'm betting the harem guards for this lot aren't eunuchs. Probably macho as fuck, with AK-47s or whatever, unless Ali decides that old-school swords work better with the scenery, or something. Sod it, let's get some supper and head back while I can still chew, yeah? I want to get the weight off my knees."

Nordine came round in front of us, and cleared his throat. "His Excellence is waiting. If you are ready...?"

He waved one hand towards the oversized front doors. No idea what they were made from, because they were open, but from the way the edges glinted where the moonlight hit them, I'd have bet on bronze.

Nordine offered his arm to Bree. I got a flash, a really strong feeling off him, that he really didn't want to, that he was only doing it because it was part of his gig. And Bree really didn't want to touch him, either; she doesn't fancy that sort of contact with strangers. But she took his arm.

Close up, the Emir's place was just as off-putting as it had been from the other end of the drive. We passed through the shiny doors and into a big open reception area. We went past that and into another open area. Beyond that, under some of the steel framing that made the place look as if it were wrongside out, we were led into a tall atrium done up as a dining room. There was a long table set with linen and crockery and whatnot, nice and formal, but in the western way—none of those fruit bowls for peeled grapes Bree'd mentioned earlier. There were two empty places at the table, side by side; every other chair was taken. From the looks of it, we were the last ones in the door.

Bree let go of Nordine's arm. He cleared his throat, and pitched his voice to carry. "Mr. and Mrs. Kinkaid."

Ali al-Wahid was sitting at the head of the table, about half a mile away it seemed like, with Carla at his left side and Patrick at his right. Carla was leaning across the table, getting in on the conversation, but she saw us and waved. Ali had been talking to Patrick and a bony pale bloke I didn't recognise, but that got his attention. He said something to the others, got up and headed our way.

"Thank you, Nordine." He was back to staring at my wife. This time, he at least remembered to swivel his head my way when he was actually talking to me. "I was told of your injury, Mr. Kinkaid. Your wife informed my staff doctor that no more than basic first aid was required. Still, I was concerned. I deeply regret that you have injured yourself while under my roof. Please, come and sit, and we will dine. Patrick Ormand and Bengt Ekberg have been going over requirements for your concert—Bengt is my own chief of security. I trust Nordine got you here in comfort?"

"Yeah, he did, ta. Nice comfy limo. Besides, it's not as if we had far to come, you know? If I hadn't trashed my knees, we could have walked."

"Indeed." He waved off a servant and held Bree's chair out for her. He'd seated us halfway down, between Luke and Domitra. "How did you come to fall?"

"Tripped over a peacock. There's quite a lot of them about, you know?"

Oh, bloody hell. I'm not sure what it was about al-Wahid that made me not want to admit a weakness, but there it was, and the words had come out with more of an edge than I'd planned. I saw Bree shoot me a look, and catch her lower lip between her teeth, biting back a faint smile.

Right. Time to get things back to some kind of normalcy. "Oi, Luke, how goes it, mate? Katia, that's a brilliant dress."

"Indeed. Well, so long as you are recovered." Ali nodded over one shoulder and headed back to his own end of the table. Luke opened his mouth, probably to ask me *never mind how I'm doing, what's all this about tripping over a peacock* but he didn't get the chance, because we got swarmed by a small regiment of servers with carts full of food. Bree was talking to Dom, but when she saw the food, her eyes got wide.

"Whoa." She leaned in so that I could hear her. The noise level in the room, all conversation and explanation of what was on the various plates, was insane. "Four kinds of caviar on one plate? Holy shit, those are black truffles! And this is just the first course. Who's he trying to impress?"

"Don't know, love. Maybe nobody. Maybe everybody." *Yeah, or maybe just you.*

I shook my head at the caviar, and Bree did the same; her feeling about getting salty fish eggs caught in her teeth runs pretty close to my own. I made sure she'd got something that worked for her—it turned out to be figs and pressed duck—and then got a few mouthfuls myself. Meanwhile, the trays just kept coming, and the food got more pricey and rarefied and fancy with every platter they trotted out. Not my thing, yeah? As soon as we got back to London, I thought, I was going out for a nice big plate of fish and chips or maybe even wrapped in newspaper, with malt vinegar on the side, and sod the bad weather.

It was a good ninety minutes before we'd belched our way through about eight courses and finished up with some sort of local sweet, with honey and nuts. Ali's army of uniformed servants whooshed through the room in a cloud of competence, clearing the table, pouring everyone tea out of huge steaming copper pots, and disappearing somewhere into the house, presumably to do a metric fuckload of washing up.

It was obvious our host wanted to give a speech, because he was standing up, tapping on his wineglass. I just hoped he'd keep it short; the stinging in my knees had gone from background to full noise, and I wasn't liking it much. They also felt damp, as if they might be leaking or oozing. Not pleasant at all, and definitely time to check the bandages...

"If I may?" Ali glanced down the table, making sure we were all paying attention. He knew how to pitch his voice to carry, I'll give him that. "I know that you are all tired. I hope you are all satisfied with your meal. I wished to say only that we are looking forward with great eagerness to the concert, and to introduce you to Bengt Ekberg. He is my Chief of Security, for anything to do with my house and my safety, here in Manaar. He will liaise and cooperate with Patrick Ormand. They have decided on the security arrangements to be put in place. Security for my old friend Malcolm is entirely at the discretion of Malcolm himself, and of course Ms. Calley. Mr. Hendry has given our grounds-keepers his list of contract requirements, in terms of space and equipment. Ms. Fanucci has signed off on the housing arrangements for all band and supplemental personnel. If there are any questions, or any objections...?"

He was looking straight at me when he asked that, and he wasn't alone, either. Most of the table had turned my way.

So, yeah, quite a lot had apparently been going on behind the scenes while I'd been getting my knees taped up and taking the nap I'd needed: the band business was taken care of, everything signed off on. Just so long as no one in the band decided to say *fuck it, don't think so mates, I'm staying home*, we were ready to rock and roll.

There was a time when not being woken up and asked for my

77

vote up front would have left me pissy enough to object out of pique. There was a time I'd have felt left out, the new kid, not important enough to ask. There was a time it would have hurt.

Those days were well behind me. I could take that much for granted these days. Just knowing that saying no would be good enough for the band to walk away from whatever was in the works, that was enough for me.

Everyone was quiet, waiting on me. Ali's speech had made it pretty clear that he'd been told upfront what our policy was: *it's all or nothing, mate, everyone or no one.*

I stood up, feeling my legs shake; Bree was up as well, one hand under my elbow in case she was needed. It was time to get our driver back. "If everyone's in, I'm in as well. Let's do it. Sorry to eat and run, but I'm not in very good shape tonight, and I need to have a lie-down. Thanks for dinner."

"(beep) JP? Hey man, it's Tony. I just wanted to let you know, we're getting there tomorrow. Carla said Sheikh Moneybags built you guys a kickass studio to rehearse in. I can't wait to see what—hang on—What? Oh! Katia says, tell Bree that if she drove that Bugatti and Katia didn't get to watch, Katia's going to kick her ass from one end of the desert to the other. Anyway, see you guys tomorrow night, unless we're snowed in and the flights are grounded. The weather in London sucks ass. Manana, guys. (beep)"

"John?" Bree was stretching, getting some yoga in. "What was that snort for?"

"Just that Katia's got a thing about that fancy car you're getting to drive. She promised you an arse-kicking if you don't wait for her to get here before you drive it. They're getting in tomorrow."

She'd been tucking herself into a lotus, but that got all her attention, and she uncoiled in a hurry. "Was that Tony? How—did he—was he—I mean –"

She stopped, and bit her lip. I grinned at her.

"No need to be delicate about it, love. He sounds fine. Nice and rested. If that's the case, the Centre and Mourdain's whole 'meditation, conversation, realisation' thing looks to have done the trick. Oi!"

She'd got up and got my face between her palms. It was a serious kiss, tongue tip to tongue tip and a bit more. The girl meant business.

"Wow." I got my breath back; both arms had got themselves round her. "What was that in aid of, lady?"

"I don't know." Her eyes had gone very green, and a bit damp. "Relief, or pride, or whatever, I don't know. Do I need a reason? John, what are you—oh, *man*…"

I don't know about Bree, but personally I was thankful for the oversized ceiling fan. It wasn't a hot night, not by Middle Eastern standards, but we generated plenty of heat on our own. After my heart attack at Wembley, Bree'd got into the habit of wanting me hard up against her long after the actual slap and tickle was done with, and that made for even more warmth.

Besides, we generally got chillier weather than the mid-seventies, most Christmas weeks, no matter whether we were in London or home in San Francisco. We'd only got back to Manaar ourselves two days ago, and my bones could still feel the London winter in them.

"Hello, darling." I had my fingers laced through hers, feeling her wedding ring against my skin. My heart was doing the fandango, wanting to argue with the tickybox, but the tickybox was winning the argument. It usually does—that's its gig. I touched my tongue to the hollow in her collarbone. "Crikey, you're a bit of a salt lick right now."

She made an incoherent little noise. It sounded like contentment, but moments like these, I can never be sure; she was still rippling away, miles away in whatever happy physical reality I'd navigated her to. I was about to try for another fifteen minutes, just taking her places and letting her ripple on, when my phone went.

I rolled off her and reached for it, and she let me. With the largest single audience we'd ever played for showing up in less than a week, I wasn't about to blow off phone calls. Bree knew that, and she knew why. The only reason I'd missed the call from Tony was because I'd been in that fancy studio Tony'd mentioned, getting some early rehearsals in and meeting with our sound and set designers about the tech. The venue for the gig was a huge park in the capital city, and with a quarter million people projected to be trotting in for this one, I wanted to know what the blokes in charge were planning.

"Hello?" I was watching my wife. She'd pulled herself upright and picked up where she'd left off on the yoga postures. This time, though, she was sitting on our bed and she wasn't wearing yoga trousers, or anything else.

"JP? It's Carla. I just wanted to let you know your interferon got here today. I'll send it over with Nordine in the morning, when he comes to pick Bree up for her lesson in the Veyron. Oh, and Tony and Katia will be here tomorrow afternoon—I told him to plan on meeting his equerry and let him know he needs to be ready to rehearse at ten the day after tomorrow. Are you okay? You sound breathless."

"I'm fine. Just a bit warm." Bree was on all fours, facing me, one leg up and stretched out behind her. The Spitting Cat, she told me that posture's called. She arched her back and lifted her head, just enough for me to see her smile through the curtain of hair. "Carla, sorry, I need to go do something. Thanks for letting me know. See you tomorrow."

I clicked the phone off and tossed it aside. Sod it. Anyone who wasn't Bree wanted me tonight, they weren't getting me.

This time, Bree actually got her land legs back before I did.

Nice to be able to surprise both of us at my age, yeah? I was still trying to get my breath back while she headed off to the loo to get my pills and one of the fancy carafes Ali's people kept us stocked with. We'd got a full suite this time, and Ali hadn't been joking when he'd told us things were being tarted up between our last visit and the show. Considering just how much tarting up had got done between the quick trip and now, either a lot of dosh had changed hands, or there was an overseer with a whip involved.

Life in the seraglio wasn't all bad, considering. Even without the peacocks, the place would have made the Four Seasons look drab.

"Here. Meds. Wow, it's nearly midnight." She pulled the silk blanket up around her waist and watched me get the pills down. "John, is it okay if I ask you something?"

That got one eyebrow up. Her feeling she needs permission to ask me questions, that's something I'd hoped had gone the way of disco and dinosaurs.

"You can ask anything you want, love. I'm surprised you don't know that by now."

"No, no, I do know." She sounded defensive, suddenly. "It's just that this is really band business, not mine. At least, I don't think it's mine. But..."

She trailed off. I waited, but nothing: she'd gone quiet. "But what? Bloody hell, your shoulders are halfway to the ceiling! What's wrong, Bree? Talk to me, please."

"Okay." She bit her lip. "We haven't talked about it since we got back here. But, well, has Patrick said anything at all about those two girls? About how security is planning on getting them to stay away from the band and the gig, I mean? I don't know if anyone even gives a shit except me, and I don't want to stick my nose in where it's got no business being, but I hate not knowing, John. I don't even know if they're still around, but every time I walk out there, I expect to see them naked in one of the pools." She shivered suddenly. "And I really don't want to see them at all."

"I don't fancy the idea much myself."

She had a point. I hadn't given the twins a second thought since we'd got back to Manaar this trip, probably because I hadn't actually seen them. Out of sight out of mind, and all that rubbish. But Bree was right, and it was something that needed dealing with, even if the only result was to put her mind at ease.

"No clue, love, but I'll check with Patrick and Bengt tomorrow. I'd ring Patrick now, but it's rather late for that." I planted a kiss on her shoulder. "It's not as if we're expecting them to climb in through the windows. Let's get some kip. You don't want to be driving that scary set of wheels if you're groggy. I've got to head over to the site in the morning anyway, before rehearsal. I'll talk to Patrick then."

Nordine showed up at ten the next morning, and this time there was no nonsense about bullet-proof limos. He was behind the wheel of the Bugatti, the first time I'd seen the thing.

I don't know a damned thing about cars. I've never learnt to drive; I manage to memorise what model Jag my wife's driving at any given moment, and that's my limit. Still, you'd have to be an idiot to look at the black and orange monster Nordine had just slid up in, and not get that this wasn't something you'd leave in the carpark while you went for a quick pint and a kebab. It looked as pricey as it actually was, and even just idling, it sounded terrifying: not really loud, but deep, as if eight thousand bass players had all hit the same note together after doing a lot of blow first. I could feel the thrum of that engine, all the way down in my belly.

Carla had made a tactical error, and nearly sent the tickybox into overdrive, by telling me how much the Veyron cost and, more to the point, how fast it went. I'd had a moment of wanting to come the heavy husband, and telling Bree I wasn't having her driving anything at over two hundred and fifty miles an hour, but I'd muffled it. For one thing, she's not a daredevil—she's a safe driver, never had an accident or even a summons for speeding. And she's my wife, not my property. However much I might have wanted to flip my shit, I don't get to order her about, you know? If she fancies driving the local dictator's supercar down a closed road as fast as she can get it to go, I'll try talking her out of it, but I don't get a vote.

That didn't mean watching her climb into the damned thing wasn't going to leave me grinding my teeth, though. It was just as well Luke and his driver had pulled in right behind the Bugatti. I had a quick silent conversation with the tickybox—*right, do your thing, she'll be fine, she's not an idiot or a kid*—snatched a quick kiss off Bree, waved her off towards Nordine, and climbed into the limo, next to Luke.

"Oi, JP. You're looking well-rested this morning."

Luke looked pretty wiped, probably from missing Karen; Bree had come out with me, but she was the only band wife there. Karen's widowed daughter Suzanne had spent Christmas at Draycote, and the current plan had Karen flying out with the rest of the wives on Boxing Day. I didn't know what Suzanne had planned, and didn't much care. I'd have been quite surprised to see her in this neck of the woods, though, considering the bad history with the al-Wahid family.

"Yeah, well, a good night's sleep'll do that." I was damned if I wanted to rub his face in me having Bree there. He wouldn't have minded—he knows better than most people just how much she does to make my life possible—but I wasn't going there. "Did you know Tony and Katia were getting in tonight? I need a word with Patrick and Bengt before we get started on anything. What exactly do they need us for today, anyway?"

"Nial probably wants us to tramp about and see if we're okay with the stage. Or maybe we're just expected to gawk at the magnificence, or something. Hell, I'm not complaining. It'll be nice to actually get a look at the venue, now that the stage is up. Besides, I could use a break from the rehearsal studio."

He yawned suddenly. "Sorry. I'm not used to the temperature difference and I don't sleep well without Karen anyway. I'll tell you what, JP, I think I'm getting old. Travel didn't used to fry me like this. Oh crikey, is this it? Are we here?"

According to all the brochures, Amina Plaza's the largest public gathering place in Manaar, and like the rest of the place, it's dead flat. As far as I could tell, Manaar's about a third the size of California, and it's shaped pretty much the same, long and skinny with a curve at the southern end. The upper part's unreclaimed coastal desert, with some oil deposits in it. Bree looked the place up online to get a better handle on it, and she'd said something about the Kalahari, in Africa.

The southern end, where the Emirate hooks out to the east, is rather different. There's plenty of sand, but it's also got things growing, and quite a sizeable freshwater river to go along with all the hot springs underground. It even gets the occasional rain shower.

The southern end is also where Ali keeps his capital city, Me-din-Manaar. About a third of it's given over to a huge green park, and huge is the word: as an open space, it'll hold three hundred thousand people with some room to spare in case of a stampede. Just as well, too, since we were expecting a quarter million to show up on New Year's Eve. It was nice to know there was room for an extra fifty thousand or so if Ali had underestimated the head count.

The Plaza's only a few minutes from the Queen's Palace by car, so there wasn't time for conversation. This was our first look at the site with the stage up, and I wasn't ready for the scale of it. Blacklight sold out Estadia Azteca in Mexico City, a hundred and five thousand screaming fans, on the Book of Days tour. We'd packed out massive stadiums from Argentina to Barcelona, but Amina Plaza was in an entirely different league.

The car pulled into the plaza from the end at the farthest point from the stage. That probably added to the sense of enormity, but the fact that the stage looked tiny from this distance really brought home just how many bodies were going to be moving about the place in just over a week.

"Jesus." Luke had got the window down for a better look. "This is the plaza? It's bloody *huge*. Christ, the stage is three hundred feet across and it looks like a puppet theatre!"

"Gordon *Bennett*!" I had the other window down; we must have looked like a pair of dogs, heads out the windows and tongues hanging out. Taking in the scale of the thing, my mouth had suddenly gone dry. "Luke, we're having video screens, right? Really big video screens, and lots of them...?"

"Yeah, we've got those." We were rolling up a long paved stretch between what looked to be miles of green lawn, and the closer we got to the stage, the bigger the area behind us looked. "I'm more worried about the seating. I know why we went with a festival setup, much easier logistics, but that's going to be one hell of a crowd with nowhere to park their bums during the slow numbers. I wish Carla hadn't headed back to LA this morning—she'd have the information at the front of her brain."

"Yeah, well, Nial or Ronan should know. Not to worry, Luke, it'll be covered. I trust the staff, you know?"

We were close enough now to see the stage layout in detail: it was smaller than our Book of Days three-circle clean-stage rig, and a lot more simple. Rather than trot our own stadium rig out of storage, we'd hired what we needed. Besides, with the size of this gig, we didn't have enough in storage to cover all the remote towers we'd need. The bill for the gear was going to be astronomical, but Carla and Ian had made sure that the rider put the full cost for any hired gear in Ali's lap. According to them, he'd signed off on that without a blink. I found myself wondering, one more time, just why the bloke was so set on having us play his little do.

Ronan, our sound designer, was waiting for us as we rolled up, with our stage designer, Nial Laybourne, right behind him. "Good, you're here. Mac's just got here, and the Bunker Brothers are setting up. Any word on Tony? I'd like you lot all up here together, to get the feel of it."

"They'll be in later, unless Heathrow's shut down for snow." Ian had come up. "Everyone's coming in today, wives, techs, the lot. We looked at the weather service projections and decided to get them all out while the going was good. Oi, chaps, you two look slackjawed. It's just a stage. Not nearly as impressive as the last one we trotted round the world."

"That's the problem. Coming in from the far end of the plaza, this thing looks like a bloody shoebox, or a kid's puppet theatre, or something." I'd been craning my neck over the hammering and lifting. "Ronan, hang on a sec, yeah? Oi! Patrick! Bengt! Can I get a word with you both, please?"

Up to that point, my contact with Bengt Ekberg had been shaking hands when we'd been introduced by Patrick, and not much else. Ali's personal muscle coordinator looked to be lacking any muscles of his own; he was so thin, he might have been designed to press all Bree's *must-feed-him* buttons. First time we'd met him, at that state dinner a couple of weeks back, I'd been too sick to give him or anything else much thought, but Dom's comment—that he looked as if the Vikings had booted him off the longboat for not meeting the minimum weight requirements for sacking Constantinople—had stuck in my head.

Now here he was, sticking out a long bony hand. I took it and shook it: nice easy grip, not trying to prove anything. He really did look underfed. Crikey, the bloke was even skinnier than I was.

"Hi, JP. How can I help you?"

"I've got a question I need to ask, for my wife. Thing is, it might be a bit delicate." I had one eyebrow up. "Sorry, but I hadn't realised you were American. Southern California?"

He grinned at me. He was so damned bony, the grin looked like a death rictus. It should have been scary, or at least off-putting, but somehow, it wasn't; it worked on him.

"Good catch. Actually, I'm pure Swede, but my father was a professor of speech pathology at UCLA. His TA used to call him Professor Potato-Eater." He lowered his voice. "Do you want to find a quiet corner? If the question is delicate, yelling it over all this noise is probably a bad move. Besides, they're setting up the first portable toilets."

I left Luke and Ian discussing video screens, and followed Patrick back behind the stage and into a trailer. It was obvious we'd borrowed the office of one of the construction bosses; there were specs and blueprints and schematics all over the desk, but the real giveaway was the corkboard on the wall behind the desk chair. It had our contract rider pinned up to it, with the tech specs for the stage at the front, all highlighted in nice bright colours, very reassuring.

"So." Bengt leaned up against the desk. "How can I help you? You said this was sensitive, JP?"

"Yeah, it is." I took a deep breath. Patrick was watching me, and I'd have laid odds he knew just what I wanted to ask, or at least who I wanted to ask about. He wasn't opening his mouth, though. Ah, sod it—might as well just say it. "It's about the al-Wahid twins. We've made it part of the deal that they can't come anywhere near the band while we're here: show, personnel, lodgings, the lot. Problem is, when we were here last, I found them skinny-dipping in the pools just outside our window."

"What?" I'd surprised Patrick, after all. "When was this, JP?"

"The day we'd first got here, and I fell and bashed up my knees. They climbed out of the damned pool, one of them in half

87

a towel and the other one stark, and giggled at me. I got the hell out of it—sorry, Bengt, I told you this was tricky, yeah? I know you work for their dad, but the truth is, those girls are bad news. There's good reasons we don't want them around."

They were both listening, not saying anything yet. I was betting Patrick had already guessed just what was coming next. He knows quite a lot about the way Bree and I work as a couple.

"Thing is, I had to tell my wife about it. Right after it happened, she was concentrating on my having got hurt, but she's got to the point now where she's afraid she's going to turn a corner and come up against one of them. I want to be able to let her know it's all right, not to worry, that won't happen. Question is, *is* it all right? Are they about? Neither of us has seen them since, but I promised her I'd find out."

"Bengt, that's your purview, not mine." Patrick sounded completely neutral, but something had flickered in his face. "I haven't seen them since I got here, JP, but of course, that doesn't prove anything—it's a big compound and we've all been working. I've got over two hundred hired security people here, but none of that touches the royal family. Bengt?"

"The daughters of the house are in residence, at home in Manaar." Out of nowhere, he sounded a lot less American, and a lot more European, or maybe Middle Eastern. Formal, you know? "They are aware that they have been barred from anything to do with the band, or with the show. They have their own quarters, under their father's roof. That you have not seen either of them since your arrival this time is no surprise. They have been instructed as to what's expected of them. They know what their duty is."

We were all quiet. Outside, people were hammering, yelling, measuring, sawing, drilling, assembling, doing what needed to happen to get the hired stage assembled and ready. In here, Patrick was watching me, and I was watching Bengt.

Something had moved in that bony face. I couldn't have said what it was, maybe annoyance at having to explain, maybe being irritated at me calling him out on something he thought was a professional issue, maybe something else entirely. I couldn't read him.

He knew I was watching him, too. He straightened up, and moved towards the door. Both of Patrick's eyebrows were up.

"Please assure Mrs. Kinkaid that the princesses won't trouble her. And now, if there's nothing else, I believe you were wanted onstage."

Chapter Six

"So, you ready to drive that thing tomorrow?"

We were spending Christmas night in Manaar just the way we might have spent it at home in San Francisco, or at the mews rental in South London: having a nice quiet supper and a serious roll-around for afters. That roll-around's the nearest thing we've got to a family tradition: no gifts, except each other. As far as I'm concerned, being able to taste salt on my wife's skin is the best present anyone could offer me anyway.

"Mmmm. I think so." She moved under me, just enough to get the edge of the tickybox under my left collarbone back where it belonged. "Nordine's coming at nine. He says it's best to take the car up to speed before the road surface gets too hot. Are you in the studio tomorrow? Or is it an outdoor rehearsal?"

"Outdoors. Now that all those damned portable toilets are set up, Ronan want to make sure there's no bounce-back issue. But I want to watch you do your drive first." I rolled over and pulled her up against me. "Happy Christmas, love."

"Liar. You do *not* want to watch, and you know it." She smiled at me, one of those smiles she never seems to produce for anyone but me. One more present, yeah? "Thank you for being such a nice husband, John. I'm going to feel better knowing you're there. No, don't freak out, I'm not really scared. That machine handles like a dream—it's actually easier to drive than the Jag, especially since I can leave it in automatic and let it do its own gear shifting. I just like knowing you're there, watching my back."

"Yeah, well, at the speed that thing gets up to, I really will be watching your back. Disappearing down the road like a damned jet, probably."

We were quiet, just curled together. Outside in the courtyard, something was singing; I had the feeling it might be a nightingale, since we were in Arabia and they've actually got them here. The fancy blue and gilt-painted grilles over the windows to our suite were open, letting the night air in.

"John? What are you doing?"

"Just relaxing." Something I've noticed the past few years, with all the travelling we'd got done: the air tastes different in different parts of the world, especially at night. In San Francisco, it depends on the time of year, but mostly it tastes of the ocean, and the fog, clean and salty. In the South of France, it tastes of flowers, the kind that bloom at night and smell almost too sweet sometimes. Here we were in Arabia, at the end of December, and the night air tasted soft and light, flowers, but not the same ones that grow in France…

"Wow, that jasmine smells amazing. I can almost taste it." Bree was murmuring into my shoulder. "Tony and Katia were really kind of neat today, weren't they? Almost like newlyweds."

"Yeah, a bit shy and careful with each other." I was beginning to drowse off; the physics of sex being what they are, I'm likely to drop off first. But she was right, there was a kind of delicacy about the Mancusos at the moment, as if, now that Tony had gone through the fire and come out the other end, they were having to relearn each other. "In a good way, though. Kind of nice to—Bree? What...?"

"Someone's in the courtyard, just outside." She'd gone stiff against me, and her voice was very quiet, too quiet. Suddenly, I wasn't sleepy anymore. "Listen."

I held my breath, keeping still myself, trying to sort out the different sounds. The nightingale was still there, singing its head off. I could hear the steady burble of the water, endlessly circulating in that collection of mineral hot pools, and the night breeze, moving in through the bars of the grilles...

"Yeah, I hear it." There it was, a soft splash, a faint quiet murmur of voices. "Sounds like someone's having a midnight dip. Could be anyone, Bree. Didn't Katia say something about wanting to make some time for a swim? Do you want me to throw some trousers on, go have a look? I will, if you want me to."

"No." She let her breath back out, and I felt her relax. Her voice was still low, but it was normal again. "Sorry. I'm being silly. You're right, it's probably Katia. If she and Tony are taking a midnight swim, I wouldn't want to disturb them. Whoa, I think I just hit the wall. Goodnight, babe."

When Bree falls asleep, she doesn't mess about. I get rather jealous of it sometimes, the way she can just decide *right, I need to be asleep now*, and off she goes, lights out and not quite snoring. I've never sorted out how she does that; even before the MS, I was iffy about sleep, and it's a lot worse these days.

So there was my wife, getting ready to drive something at two hundred fifty miles an hour in the morning, off to dreamland within two minutes of telling me goodnight. Unfortunately, I was nowhere near sleep. Maybe it was the taste of jasmine on the air, maybe it was too much coming up in the near future, or maybe I was more worried about the drive of hers than I was letting on to myself. Whatever it was, my brain was too busy to let go straight off. From the edge of sleep, I'd woken up.

Six days to go, and Blacklight would be playing the biggest show we'd ever done. We weren't the first band to headline a gig to a crowd this size, not by any stretch—the Stones had done it more than once. But I couldn't shrug and say, *right, just another gig*. It wasn't.

If I'd had any inclination to try and shrink the scope of the show in my head, the portable toilets had set me straight: there were over two thousand of the damned things, and tankers were being brought in to keep them usable. Stu Corrigan had taken one look at them being unloaded, lorry after lorry after lorry, and summed it up quite nicely: *Fuck me, that's a lot of crappers.*

Bree sighed and turned over, snuggling deeper into her pillows. The silk sheet was still down round her waist, but it wouldn't be long before she'd be reaching for it, pulling it up round her shoulders and burrowing in hard. The room was still warm, but it was going to cool off quite a lot over the next couple of hours. We'd learned that much about the Arabian nights: when the temperature drops, it goes fifteen degrees or more, and it does it quick.

Ali's interior designers had left his Gran's windows where they were, just slightly beyond what's comfortable for me to reach. All they'd done was touch up the paint and gilt, and added decent locks and a longish hook stick thing to pull things together with. They hadn't enlarged them, either—they probably felt long skinny short windows with shiny grilles on them added to the ambience, or something. Dealing with them was a nuisance, and normally Bree would have shut them, since she's got two inches on me and a longer reach as well. Tonight, we'd been busy making Christmas merry, and we'd both forgotten.

The chill of that desert temperature drop nailed me as soon as I slid out from under the silk. Funny thing: with the colder air, the taste and smell of it changed. There didn't seem to be quite as much jasmine in the mix anymore, and it wasn't as sweet, somehow.

I headed over toward the casement, shivering like a puppy in a thunderstorm. Right. Grab the damned hook, no fumbling about, pull the grilles shut and down and get the fuck back under the covers and next to my nice warm wife...

Maybe the room was quieter than I'd thought. Maybe the breeze had died down. All I know is, the splash from outside sounded too loud. It wasn't the soft light noise that had got Bree to stiffen up—this was deeper, fuller, heavier. And there were no soft murmurs now. What I was hearing through the open grille sounded more like the slap of bare feet against the ground. Someone was running.

I set the stick back down. Maybe I've seen a bit too much these past few years, enough to get paranoid, or maybe my sensors are just permanently cocked open. Whatever—I don't know. The bottom line was, my heart was pushing the tickybox into overdrive. Every instinct I've got was yelling at me.

I got into my trousers as quickly and quietly as I could manage it. Bree was fathoms deep. Good; I was damned if I wanted her waking up and having to deal with anything in the way of trouble. I got my shoes on, and threw on one of the silk robes that came with the suite. I must have looked a complete git, designer shoes and a bathrobe straight out of Central Casting's idea of a Rudolph Valentino film.

Room keys, lock the door behind me, out into the corridor. Odd thing, the way the shadows along the walls seemed to move so much out here...

"Johnny?"

"Mac, for fuck's sake!" I managed to keep it to not much more

94